The crop flipped out of Lucy's hand, but the fall was perfect. She huddled on the ground trying to appear unconscious until Van yelled, *"Cut."* When she looked up, the snake was slithering toward her.

He's defanged, Lucy reminded herself. It's only J.R., probably frightened by the crop. She was mesmerized as the long forked tongue whipped up and down and the whir of the rattle magnified in her ears. Suddenly, the snake coiled again and raised its head straight in the air. In an instant it lunged across several feet to land open-mouthed against Lucy's leg.

It withdrew as fast as it had struck.

Lucy stared at her chap.

"Help!" she yelled. "Somebody come *quick!*"

CLAIRE BIRCH has written and produced many well-known documentaries on a variety of subjects. She lives in New York City.

A Lucy Hill Mystery #3

Double Danger

Claire Birch

Published by
Dell Publishing Co., Inc.
1 Dag Hammarskjold Plaza
New York, New York 10017

Laurel-Leaf Library ® TM 766734, Dell Publishing Co., Inc.

ISBN: 0-440-92126-0

RL: 5.4

Printed in the United States of America

First printing—October 1985

For Nathan—East Coast or West

Chapter One

Lucy found it hard to believe that she was looking at herself in familiar riding clothes—the canary breeches and high black boots, the polo shirt and hunt cap—when everything else was so extraordinary. This wasn't her bedroom mirror in New York. She was standing in the wardrobe department of a Hollywood studio.

"That green shirt really matches your eyes," Lynne said. Lynne Stokes, assistant producer of her father's television show, had driven Lucy to the studio.

Lucy stared into the mirror. Her brown hair still reached to her shoulders. Her face was still long and oval. How could she look just the same when she felt so different?

"Does Darci Rutland have her riding things yet?"

The wardrobe woman threaded a belt through the loops on Lucy's breeches. "Darci's due here any minute," she said. "Since you're doubling for her, your clothes are exactly the same."

Lucy had been dying to meet Darci for two whole days, ever since stepping off the plane in Los Angeles. She looked at Lynne hopefully.

"I wish we could hang around, Lucy, but your father will be waiting to have lunch with us back at the house."

"We're finished," the wardrobe woman said, moving a pin at the back of Lucy's collar. "I'll bring all your clothes to Malibu on Wednesday."

"Thanks. Everything looks great."

In the dressing room, Lucy changed back into her own pants and shirt and was glad for a few minutes to herself. No matter how cool she tried to seem, a costume fitting for a TV show was exciting. And everything had been in high gear from the moment she'd arrived in California. Since her parents had separated nine months ago, Lucy had been living with her mother in New York. Meanwhile, after years of making commercials in the East, her father had come to Hollywood to produce a television series. From August to March Lucy had only seen her father two Sundays in New York. These two weeks over spring vacation were supposed to give them some time together. And as a special treat, Mr. Hill had arranged for Lucy to do the riding scenes in one of his *Malibu* episodes.

Lucy stalled a bit, still hoping to get a look at Darci, but finally she had to give up. Fifteen minutes later she and Lynne drove past the studio guard and maneuvered onto the freeway.

"Just how much do I really look like Darci?" Lucy said, putting on her sunglasses and gazing at the soft mountains in the distance.

"Darci's eyes are brown, not green, and she does look older. You're almost sixteen, right? Well, Darci's twenty. But there's an amazing resemblance. To tell the truth, I think that's why your father hired her."

"Come on, Lynne."

"I've thought so from the beginning. And they've gone on writing her into one episode after the other. First she was only supposed to be in for one week. Now we're up to eight. Darci's not a big star, after all."

"Of course she is! Everyone knows Darci Rutland. She was a star when I was little."

"Sure. But as they say out here, 'what's she done lately?' Sweet little Darci, America's darling, wasn't such a cute adolescent." Lynne smiled at Lucy. "The teens haven't hurt *your* looks any. It's good to see you, Lucy."

"You, too. I've always remembered how nice you were to me whenever I came to Dad's office." And your spectacular red hair, Lucy thought. And discovering that a face covered with freckles could still be beautiful.

"But you were only about eight when I moved out here."

"I remember that, too. You married a cameraman."

Lynne nodded. "When did you get so serious about riding? It must have been after I left."

"About two years later. That's the toughest thing about living in New York with my mother—it's too far to commute to Mr. Kendrick. He's my riding teacher at Up and Down Farm in Connecticut."

"But can't you ride in New York?"

"No place where I can get the training I need. I'm trying to get to the Maclay Trophy finals at the National Horse Show and that's the toughest competition there is. I've just started riding at Oak Ridge stables in

9

Westchester, and next summer, well . . . maybe we'll be back in Connecticut."

"You mean you and your mom?"

Lucy thought a minute. What *did* she really mean?

"I guess I mean all of us. I don't know if Dad's going to stay out here forever. Maybe he'll hate it. Besides, this separation is just to try things out."

Lynne was quiet and the hum of the car engine sounded louder than before. Lucy looked at the radiant day beyond the car window. Puffs of white clouds hung motionless against a brilliant sky. The light in California seemed to have an extra sparkle. The flowers were especially vivid—even the lawns and hedges were the greenest she'd ever seen.

"How was your stunt lesson yesterday?" Lynne said suddenly. "For you, falling off a horse must be harder than staying on."

"I'm black and blue, but I should get the hang of it by the time we shoot the scene." Lucy laughed. "It's funny how out here you can plan on filming on Monday for sure. Back home Dad always worried about rain wrecking the schedule."

"We don't have much rain in L.A., but still we've endless ways to get off schedule. Today we lost the morning because your Dad and Van Fortune, our director, had to testify at a union hearing."

"How come?"

"A problem with a special-effects man. I'm sure you'll hear all about it at lunch."

They left the freeway and climbed the low mountains separating the Valley from Beverly Hills and Hollywood. As the road twisted and turned, Lucy stared at the odd houses jutting out from the side of the canyon. Who would want to sleep in a room that was propped up with nothing but stilts?

"So tell me more about last weekend," Lynne said. "Didn't your grandparents come down from Santa Barbara? I'll bet they were pleased to see you."

"Yeah. I mean, yes. But I'm not too thrilled with them right now. They're so happy to have my father out here, they don't realize how tough it is on Mom and me."

"What about your brother? Is he as upset about the separation as you are?"

"He's away at college, so we don't talk much. But if you remember Eric, he never gets as intense about things as I do."

The road began to descend into Benedict Canyon, where Lucy's father lived. After several minutes Lynne spoke slowly and carefully. "Your Dad's missed you dreadfully, Lucy, and producing this series means lots of pressure. Why not just have a good time together while you're out here. Put your family problems on hold. It's hard for you, I know, but it would be best for everyone."

They were approaching her father's house, a small stuccoed retreat tucked against the canyon behind a lattice of leaves and vines.

Lynne's probably right, Lucy thought. Why spoil my time out here when there's nothing I can change. But what did Lynne mean by everyone? Why did it seem as though she was including herself?

"Have something to eat, Lucy." Mr. Hill pointed to the platter of delicatessen sandwiches in the middle of the table. "How did it go this morning?"

"Everything was perfect. I'd sure like that pair of breeches for the spring horse shows."

"I'll talk to the producer. Somehow I think he'll say yes." Her father broke into a smile.

Lucy reached for a tuna fish sandwich and studied him carefully. His smile was subtle and charming, not full of teeth and spread all over his cheeks. His bony face looked thinner than she remembered and there was definitely gray hair among the black. But his blue eyes seemed brighter than ever.

"It's going to be a rough week," Mr. Hill said. "If I seem to forget about you, don't believe it. Delivering twenty-six shows in a row is a workout."

"Don't worry, Dad. I expected you'd be busy."

Lynne put a bowl of salad on the table and sat down.

"Now about the riding," Mr. Hill said. "I hope you and Timon are keeping it all simple. He's one of the most responsible stuntmen in the business, but still, I don't want you to take any crazy chances."

He waved a small cardboard square. "Do you know what this is? Your membership card in the Screen Actors Guild."

Lucy reached out eagerly, but her father put the card under his plate. "Hold on. I want a promise first. Timon is used to working with pros. If he gets carried away, I want you to tell me."

"Dad, I've got three scenes, right? One's just putting a horse in a stall. And the chase scene's no worse than racing across a field. Okay, the snake scene's trickier. The horse rears at the snake and I fall off. But I fall off sometimes at Mr. Kendrick's too."

"Not often from a rearing horse!"

"Yeah, but I wear padding and Timon's shown me exactly what to do. There's a special step thing above the stirrup on one side of the saddle. I push off and then it's like tumbling in gym."

Mr. Hill frowned and rubbed the back of his neck.

"Don't look like that, Dad. You've always let me do hard things if I could learn to do them right. Don't back off now."

"So I had an attack of cold feet. Just remember, you may be Darci's double in the credits but for me you're the star of the show." His eyes caught hers. "You know that, don't you?"

"Sure!"

The doorbell rang.

"That's probably Van," Mr. Hill said. "We've a production meeting at two thirty and he's always early."

As Mr. Hill left the table Lucy thought back to her weekend sessions with Timon. Her father didn't have to know that she was a patchwork of bruises. She'd been careful not to wince when she sat down! She was going to do those scenes no matter what.

For the fall, Timon had taught her to free her feet from the stirrups, grab the horse's mane, and push off with her head tucked against her chest. "How high you let the horse rear before you fall will tell us how brave you are," he'd said. She'd show them.

A tall thin light-haired man joined them at the table and her father introduced Lucy to Van Fortune, the

13

Malibu director. Lynne handed Van a cup of coffee. "Well, gentlemen," she said, "did Jake show up sober?"

"As far as anyone could tell," Van answered.

"That's the thing about Jake. You *can't* tell." Mr. Hill turned to Lucy. "Jake Hemmings is a special-effects man who worked for us on the first few shows. We've brought him up on negligence charges because of an accident on the set."

"In one episode," Lynne explained, "the script called for a bomb in Paul Martin's car. He's the evil grandson played by Mark Ladd. It was Jake's job to set the timer on the bomb so that it would explode at the right moment—"

"And it didn't?" Lucy blurted out.

"Far from it. We claim Jake had been drinking, got mixed up in his counts, and set the timer incorrectly." Mr. Hill took over. "Mark testified that he'd rehearsed the scene at least five times—that he was supposed to get out of the car, cross in front of it, and reach the steps of the house before the explosion. We showed them the take, and anyone with one eye could see that Mark was just closing the car door when the blast went off."

"A second sooner," Van said, "and he'd have been burned, instead of singed."

"Mark Ladd was actually burned? So how could Jake have any defense?" Lucy said.

"He laid it on *me.*" Van's words were sharp-edged.

For the first time, Lucy looked at Van closely. He seemed a few years older than her father—about fifty. His dark blond hair was streaked with platinum and his skin was bronze enough for a suntan lotion commercial. A patterned ascot around his neck was tucked into a lavender sport shirt.

"There were no surprises," Van said. "He had a tough, smart lawyer and they played the tune Jake's been piping all over town—the blast went off too early because I gave him the wrong timings."

"That's absurd," Lynne said.

"Jake insisted I blocked the scene one way and shot it another," Van went on. "He left in a rage, cursing out Allan for wrecking his reputation and swearing to get even. He said—"

"We'll hear in a week or two," Mr. Hill broke in quickly. "The Inquiry Committee will have to refer its decision to the union council."

"What does all this do to your production, Dad?"

"Nothing in particular. I just couldn't let that guy get away with sheer recklessness on a show of mine. I may be the new boy on the block, but I had to press charges."

Mr. Hill pushed back his chair. "We'd better get to work. There are a few things to go over with Lynne and Van before the rest of the gang shows up." He kissed Lucy on the top of her head. "Our production manager is bringing a stack of tapes from the office so you can immerse yourself in *Malibu*. But, 'Warning: Large Dosages May Be Fatal.' They're made to be seen one show at a time."

"Terrific, Dad. Forget about me."

"If we get finished early enough, I'll drive you out to Timon for another lesson," her father said.

That wasn't a good idea at all. Time enough for her

15

father to see the rear and fall the day of the shoot. Then he couldn't stop her.

"I don't think Timon expects me today," Lucy said. "We'll see."

Mr. Hill settled down at one end of the living room with Van and Lynne. Lucy figured she might as well clear the table. As she brought the lunch dishes to the kitchen she almost felt she was back in their old house in Connecticut doing an everyday chore. But there was no trace of her mother here at all. This house was rented, but it was obviously her father's. The furniture was a mixture of styles. Books and scripts were stacked around, and he'd added new pieces of Mexican folk art. Her mother liked things to match, and her books were always put back on the shelves. Still, her house would be filled with bright color, fresh flowers, and the modern art that she liked.

As more people arrived for the meeting, Lucy parked herself in front of the VCR. She watched three *Malibu* shows in a row. It was fun to hear bits of conversation from the other end of the room about the fate of the characters on the screen.

The main part in *Malibu* was Calloway Martin, widow of the powerful head of Magnum Studios. Week after week she struggled to retain control of her husband's entertainment empire. Gradually Lucy sorted out Calloway's two sons and their collection of wives, ex-wives, and girlfriends. There was also a favorite grandson, Paul. Played by Mark Ladd, he was twenty years old, absolutely evil, and gorgeous.

At last the meeting began to break up and people drifted toward her. Lynne came and looked at the screen with Lucy. "Mark's as nice as he is handsome," she said.

"I still haven't seen Darci."

"I guess not. She's Paul Martin's half sister, who shows up from the East—but not until episode five."

Mr. Hill came over with Van. "I'm delighted to see you're still conscious, Lucy."

"You bet I am. You've got *Dallas* and *Falcon Crest* beat by a mile."

"You'll meet the cast and the key production people tomorrow. We're moving into Van's house at Malibu for the rest of the week. We'll be nearer the set, and have a few days at the beach too. Van's throwing a party tomorrow night—I suspect in your honor."

A young woman with wispy blond hair and huge brown eyes came up to Mr. Hill. "This must be Lucy," she said.

"Right. Priscilla Jones, our script supervisor; Lucy Hill, my daughter."

"Hi, Lucy. Have you been studying your look-alike?"

"She hasn't turned up yet."

Priscilla peered at Lucy. "You *do* look a lot like her. Van, isn't it amazing? Anyway, Lucy, if twenty-year-old Darci gets to be too much, I can show you what she was like at seven—in *The Little Soldier,* her biggest hit."

"Really? I saw it ages ago. I'd love that!"

"Count me in," Lynne said.

"Well, chickadee," Van said, "you'll meet Darci in person soon enough. And if she doesn't behave herself, we'll just let you double for her altogether. Would you like that?"

"I'll settle for the riding, uh—Mr. Fortune."

"It's Van, sweetheart. Van."

Priscilla laughed. "Lucy, don't turn down Van's offer until you meet Mark."

If only she could think of a line. Pretend you're Allison, she told herself. Her New York friend Allison could always think of an answer.

"I thought Mark played Darci's brother," she said. "Doesn't that sort of limit the possibilities?"

"On-screen, maybe. Not off." Priscilla waved. "Bye. See you at Malibu."

"Right."

Mr. Hill went to the television set. "Sorry, honey, we have to look at this audition tape. Watch it with us. There's an actress Van wants to use in an upcoming show."

As the tape began to roll, Van, Lynne, and Mr. Hill watched intently. As they talked about the actress's "presence" and "projection," Lucy's attention wandered to her father. His eyes were fixed on the screen, his body alert with concentration. He was really having a good time out here, just as confident about making a Hollywood TV series as he'd been about one-minute commercials in New York. And Lynne was right in there with him, once again part of the team. It was hard to watch. Would he ever come back home? Still, Lucy could understand in a way. His California life was exciting. She thought so, too!

Chapter Two

Lucy's eyes moved from the stretch of ocean on their left to Mark's profile as he watched the road. It felt totally unreal to be sitting beside this incredibly handsome guy—a movie star—and driving up the Pacific Coast Highway to Malibu in a silver Porsche.

Her father and most of the production unit were on location in L.A., but Mark had been free to work with her on the big chase scene for the first time. Lynne had arranged for them to drive together to Oceanbluff—the tennis and riding club where they would be filming for the next few days. Everyone would regroup at Van's house around seven.

Mark changed the tape in the car stereo and soft rock filled the car. Lucy took a deep breath and started counting backward from one hundred by sevens. She could usually put herself to sleep that way at night. Maybe it would help her to keep her head.

"I'll be staying in Malibu this week too," Mark said. "Maybe you and your father could come over to dinner one night."

"I thought you live in Beverly Hills? Isn't your father Kirk Ladd, the actor?"

"Yes to both. But my folks have a place at the beach and Rita's there now."

"Rita's your mother?"

"No, my mother died when I was little. But Rita's been a great stepmother. I think your Dad knows her. Rita Royden. She's head of the story department at Roxford Productions."

Mark was about the best-looking guy she'd ever seen, with deep brown eyes and curling lashes, wavy brown hair, a fantastic straight nose and a strong chin. Lucy looked away. Calm *down.* She had to think of him as a person. Then he'd get to know her better too.

The intense sun cast a golden sheen on everything in sight, even the scruffy hills to the right of the road. The land beyond rose in ridges and valleys to the Santa Monica Mountains in the distance.

"It must be fun to ride through those canyon trails. I guess you've done it a lot," Lucy said.

"From the time I was a kid. But now I keep a horse at the Equestrian Center in L.A. I've got a great trainer there, Doreen Ambling. You should see that setup before you leave. It's really something."

The seat belt tightened against Lucy's shoulder as she turned to Mark. "I knew you rode well enough to do your own scenes for my Dad, but you're a *serious* rider."

"I bought a really talented jumper last year, so I guess I qualify. And we kept a little show pony here in Malibu until I was ten."

"At Oceanbluff?"

"Yes. Most people belong for the tennis or the swimming pool, but they've had a good stable there for years. It's not just a place that rents plugs to take up into the mountains."

"I did see some beautiful horses. But from the looks of Timon, I wasn't sure this stable was turning out polished riders."

"Timon doesn't work at Oceanbluff. He's a stunt guy who trains horses and riders for films. While we work at the club, he's been allowed to keep some horses there."

"Have you worked with him before?"

"A few times. Timon's okay."

"You sound as though you don't like him."

"He knows what he's doing. Leave it at that."

"I've read the scene we're going to work on. You try to push me into the canyon!"

"Yeah, you'll see. I'm pretty rotten." Mark took his eyes from the road and looked straight at Lucy for a second. "To tell you the truth, I'm surprised your father let you get into this."

"He thought I'd have fun. And I will."

"I hope so." They drove along without speaking.

Lucy looked out the window. What had he meant by "I hope so." Surely he'd been kidding.

Mark pointed toward the ocean. "Here's where the Malibu Colony begins. A lot of big stars have houses inside that fence. We live there too," he added.

Lucy wasn't interested in houses right now. She turned back to the hills and canyons across the road. This wasn't Connecticut, with its broad fields and level trails. But so what. Riding was riding. Or was it?

And Mark was an even bigger question. What kind

of a guy was he? She wasn't going to let him think he'd scared her.

"Mark, doesn't Darci play a pretty rotten character in this series too?"

"You bet."

"Okay," Lucy said. "I think I can give back what I get."

Pretty lame, but Mark looked startled. Lucy turned back to the window, hiding a smile.

Even from a distance, Timon's huge shoulders and large square head looked clumsy and out of proportion, as he stood on the ridge above the trail. Lucy and Mark held their horses steady as he called down instructions.

"Remember, the camera's going to be up here looking down on you guys. We'll work this out one part at a time. You turn around, Lucy, and move back until I tell you to quit."

Lucy turned Durkin quickly and trotted off in the direction Timon pointed. She felt comfortable with the wiry brown horse; she'd been riding him for the last three days. His mouth was less sensitive than she liked, not as responsive to her hands, but that was just as well if she and Mark were going to push and shove each other around.

"Farther Lucy. The camera can still see you."

"There's a fork in the trail here, Timon. Which side should I take?"

"The ocean side, on your right."

Lucy moved to the right until she saw the water.

Riding horseback with mountains on one side and the sea on the other was, for her, a spectacular first.

"Can you hear me, Lucy?" Timon yelled.

"Just barely," she shouted.

"Okay, pick out some landmarks so you can get to that same place again."

Lucy spotted a lopsided bush on one side of the trail and an outcropping of rocks on the other.

"Now," Timon continued, "walk back toward me at an easy pace."

"Hold it!" Timon called when Lucy was directly below him. "Mark will gallop Haywire toward you so that you meet right there. He'll run right up against you, and your horse is supposed to bolt. Make Durkin take off and run around the side of the hill. Mark will give chase, catch up, and try to edge you off the trail. He'll come at you three times and each time you'll shove him away. Durkin's done this before, so don't worry. He can get his feet back under him even if you pitch into the ravine."

Thanks, Lucy said to herself. She wet her lips.

"Ladd, have you got that?" Timon called to Mark, who was calming his large chestnut horse.

"Got it."

"Then try it first at a trot."

As Mark rode toward her, Lucy tightened her grip on the saddle and shortened her reins. Mark pressed Haywire against Durkin's side and Lucy trotted off in the direction of the ravine.

"Lucy, you're not pushing back," Timon yelled. "Fight him off. Mark, use your leg on the side away from the camera to move Haywire away from Durkin."

Haywire really seemed about to live up to his name as he snorted and tried to toss his head, but Lucy did her best to run Durkin up against him. Each time Mark gave way. Aside from flicking his ears from time to time, Durkin showed no reaction whatever.

"Now hold it," Timon yelled. "I'm coming down to show you how to end the scene."

"I'm glad I read the script," Lucy said to Mark as she looked at the drop below. "I remember that we both get away."

"I wouldn't be sure," Mark said. "They rewrite these things all the time."

Timon slid down the last part of the hill and strode toward them. "Okay. Now the thing is, Lucy, you've got to escape from Mark in a way that really looks good. You'll have to let Durkin know exactly what you want. If you pull back on him all of a sudden, Mark will still be moving forward. As soon as he's out in front, you can wheel around and go like blazes."

"What happens to Mark?" Lucy asked.

"He wheels around, too, but the horse rears and throws him."

"And I get away?"

"Yeah."

They walked through the ending several times, then Timon sent Lucy back to her mark. "All right, this time let's go for broke," he shouted.

Lucy brushed a few flies from Durkin's neck and nudged the horse into a fast walk. "You won't let me down now, Durkin, will you?" She spoke out loud, then started to laugh. What she'd really meant was "Don't let me down into the ravine."

An hour later Lucy was thirsty and hot, the horses were lathered, but Timon was still shouting for more action or different timing.

"Timon," Mark called suddenly, "what if we work on this some more another day?"

"Going soft on me, Ladd? I'm surprised."

Lucy saw Mark's face go white.

"Is there something I'm not doing right?" Lucy asked quickly.

"You both look as though you're still walking through it. That's why we like to work with pros instead of amateurs. They get paid to make it count. Are you going to try it again?"

Mark trotted back to his starting position without an answer.

"Of course," Lucy said loudly.

Lucy walked along the path at Timon's cue. This time she tried to put herself into Darci's part, to make herself feel like Jessica, Paul Martin's half sister, out for a ride with no hint of danger. When Mark came at Lucy she was unprepared for the force with which Haywire hit Durkin. She lost her left stirrup as the horse took off at a gallop. Haywire pounded along behind her to where the trail ran close to the ravine.

Before Lucy could bring Durkin under control, Haywire pressed up against him as though Mark had no intention of backing off. Mark's face was twisted and mean. Was this still acting or was it deadly serious? Though the dangling stirrup made it harder, Lucy threw all her weight away from the ravine and yanked Durkin's head to the side. She shoved her horse against Haywire, kicking out at the same time with the leg nearest Mark. At last he gave way. But there were still two more encounters ahead.

Quickly, Lucy slid her foot back into the stirrup before Mark could make his next move. As he crowded her off the trail, she joined her weight with Durkin's to thud against Haywire's side. It was useless. Haywire rammed up against her, moving them both off the trail toward the edge of the hill.

"You can't get away with this," Lucy yelled, putting both reins in her outside hand and slamming her free arm across Mark's chest. Mark moved Haywire to the center of the path, but as they raced along side by side, his face was contorted with anger. Lucy was ready as he charged again. Before the horses could collide, she pulled Durkin back to a stop. She wheeled around and galloped back along the trail to finish the scene. High above her Timon shouted, "That's it, Lucy. You looked like you meant it. Okay, we can quit."

Past the fork in the rail, out of sight, Lucy brought Durkin to a stop. She was breathing hard. What was that all about? She wiped a sleeve across her eyes. What kind of a Dr. Jekyll and Mr. Hyde character was Mark anyway? He owed her an answer.

Lucy leaned against the wooden railing of Van's sun deck with a plate of food in her hand. A table nearby was covered with a Mexican cloth and spread with an elaborate buffet. It seemed as if all the people she'd met on the television screen yesterday were acting in a new program in front of her.

Mark was talking to a handsome older woman whose strong, youthful face was framed by a pageboy of perfectly white hair. Lucy recognized Slade Porter, star of dozens of feature movies, and now Calloway Martin in *Malibu*. There she was, no more than twenty feet away, and all Lucy had to do was to walk up and say hello. It would be obnoxious to ask for an autograph tonight, but she'd look for a chance before the week was out.

As Mark moved away from Slade, Lucy wondered if he'd come and say hello. Not that she really wanted to talk to him. But in a way, she did. After rehearsing the scene, they'd returned the horses to the barn and driven to Van's with hardly a word to each other. This guy was really a puzzle. Which side of him should she believe?

Mr. Hill came from the living room toward the table.

"Hello, honey," her father said. "What are you doing out here alone? Let me get some food and we'll make the rounds together."

"I'm having a great time gorging on crabmeat." She looked across the room. "Dad, who's that man with the beard and the steel-rimmed glasses talking to Slade?"

"Ross Rubell, the Director of Photography."

"You really picked a winner for the star of your show. I think Slade's the most beautiful older woman I've ever seen."

"Come with me. I'll introduce you to her."

"Later, okay? I'm still hungry."

Now Mark was talking to Priscilla, the script supervisor. Every so often he broke into a charming grin. Maybe he'd been caught up in his part that afternoon. Lucy wondered if maybe she'd been seeing the face of Paul Martin, Calloway's rotten, grasping grandson. Or was there a nasty streak under all this perfection?

Drop it, Lucy told herself. Just ignore the guy. You'll only know him for two weeks anyway.

A young woman was poised at the entrance to the living room as if waiting to be noticed. At last! This had to be Darci Rutland. When no one looked up, she glided through the living room, head cocked to one side and a fixed smile on her face. She greeted Slade with an effusive hug and scattered kisses in a trail across the room. Lucy noticed a small overstuffed woman and a tall reedlike man straggling behind her.

This was Darci, all right. How could anyone possibly think that she, Lucy, resembled this sophisticated person in the purple and white jumpsuit, carefully made up even to the perfect violet eye shadow.

Darci stepped out onto the sun deck. "Hey, you're Lucy. Allan's daughter."

Lucy put her fork on her plate and held out her hand, but Darci leaned past it and kissed Lucy's cheek. "Aren't I the lucky one. I've got such a cute little twin!" Her smile widened. "I know we're going to have a great time."

Lucy stiffened. Before she could think of something friendly to say, Darci took off.

"Van, Van darling, how terrific of you to get us all together like this. It was such a nice thing to do for Allan's daughter."

Lucy turned to the ocean. It was getting darker and

a spill of moonlight lay across the water like a silver landing strip for the gulls circling above it.

A tinkling sound made Lucy turn back to the house. At the center of the living room, Van was swinging a set of oriental brass bells. "Everyone's here now, chickadees. Time for my news and the bubbly, too. Grab a glass, everybody!"

The corks began to pop, and Van, helped by Ross and Priscilla, made sure that everyone held a goblet of champagne.

Van raised his glass. "First, of course, we'll drink to Lucy, who's spending her vacation watching us work."

Vacation? Lucy rubbed the bruise on her hip from the weekend's practice. She managed a wide smile as glasses were raised in her direction.

"Now for the stunner," Van went on. "Thanks to all of you, the news got around that old Van was better than ever." He bowed in appreciation to the left and the right. "The papers were signed at noon today. The gossip columns haven't even guessed. But who do you think is going to direct Roxford Productions' multibuck new feature, *Not in the Stars?*"

As congratulations exploded across the room there was a voice at Lucy's shoulder. "You *do* look like my Darci. Not exactly, of course, but I see what everyone means." It was the woman who had arrived with Darci. She indicated the tall thin man. "This is Ray Toone, Darci's stepfather. I'm her mother, as you probably guessed."

"I'm glad to meet you," Lucy said automatically. "You too, Mr. Toone." She looked closely at the woman beside her, who was holding a plate heaped with food. In spite of the rolls of fat her face was surprisingly pretty.

Suddenly Darci's mother pulled at her husband's sleeve. "Ray, look at Darci. What should I do?"

Darci was doubled over in a chair, clutching her stomach. No one else seemed to have noticed, but Lynne was hurrying over. She helped Darci up and began to lead her in the direction of the bathroom.

Mr. Toone put a hand on his wife's arm. "It's all right, Mavis. Just stay calm and let Lynne handle it. We'll see what happens."

Probably just some kind of cramp, Lucy thought. Nothing to fuss about. But Darci was certainly pale— as white as the empty china plate Lucy still held in her hand.

Chapter Three

An hour later Darci still looked pale and exhausted. But sprawled out on a couch near Lucy, she insisted she was fine. Van had invited her to stay overnight so she'd be nearer the location for the 7:00 A.M. cast call. Lucy wasn't thrilled about sharing her room, but there wasn't any choice.

"Good night everyone. Feel better, Darci." Slade stepped out into the night, making her exit a special event.

Lynne was close behind. "Great party, Van. Good-bye all!"

Lucy studied Lynne thoughtfully. Somehow she could just put on a plain silk shirt with a few crazy beads and look like someone in a magazine.

"Great news, Van," Ross, the Director of Photography, said at the door. "Your new film will be a block-buster—even bigger than the book."

Darci leaned toward Lucy and whispered, "He's already trying to line up the picture for himself."

"How do you mean?"

"Get Van to hire him, of course."

"He seemed to be really happy for Van."

"Don't be naive."

I'd rather be naive than as cynical as you, Lucy thought. "Will you be in Van's picture?" Lucy asked.

"Yes," Darci said. "At least, I'd better be."

Van clapped his hands in front of them. "To bed, chickadees. The whole idea of the girl's dormitory was to have my starlet rested and full of evil for the big pool scene tomorrow."

"Oh, is Darci staying here?" Suddenly Mavis was hovering nearby. "Will you be all right, Darci?"

"Of course. Quit it, Mavis, *please.*"

"I'm still 'Mother' to you, miss. It's six more months before you can tell me off."

Darci looked uncomfortable. "Not here, Ma. Look, I'll be okay. Why don't you come to the shoot tomorrow."

Mrs. Toone's face lit up. "Did you hear that, Ray? We'll be there, honey. I always know your lines. I can help you go over them."

"Good night, then." Darci stood up. "Where do we sleep, Lucy? The director's sent us to bed."

"At the end of the hall."

"Do you want a wake-up call, Lucy?" Mr. Hill asked.

"It's okay, Dad. There's an alarm clock in our room."

"Would you like some juice to take with you?"

"No thanks, Dad."

"Well then, I guess there's nothing I can do for you." He sounded forlorn. "Good night, honey."

Lucy went back and hugged her father hard.

"I hope this is working out for you, Mite," he said in her ear. She hated to have him use that little-girl name in front of people, but he hadn't forgotten once so far. Right now, she was glad to hear him say it just for her.

"It really feels good to be part of your life out here. It's great." She added softly, "Honest, you don't need to fuss over me—you'll double for Darci's mother." They both laughed, and Lucy followed Darci down the hall.

In the guest room, Darci dropped her purse onto one of the twin beds and went into the bathroom. She certainly takes over, Lucy thought, starting to undress.

"Darci, do you feel okay?" she called out after a while.

"Yeah. I've got the shakes, that's all." Darci came back into the room. "I'm cold. I don't suppose you could lend me a nightgown."

"Sure." Lucy took a cotton nightshirt from her suitcase. "Do you have a virus or something?"

"No. Nothing like that." Darci pulled the nightshirt on over her head and sat down on the bed. She cocked her head to one side. "I'd like to tell you, but I'm afraid you'll tell your father."

"Not if it's none of his business."

"Well, it's not. And I may be crazy. But I think someone drugged my champagne tonight. That's why I threw up."

"Come on, Darci."

"No, listen! There was something in my glass that was supposed to make me a whole lot sicker than I was."

33

"Why do you say that?" Lucy tried not to show any surprise.

"I remember thinking it was really rotten champagne—not the stuff Van usually serves. I knocked over the glass by mistake. Ask Mark. He was with me. More than half the drink spilled, or I'd be out cold right now, getting my stomach pumped."

"You sound like a script for *Malibu*. Who would want to knock you out?"

After several minutes it was clear that Darci wasn't going to answer. Lucy reached into her suitcase for the toilet kit her mother had bought for her to take on this trip. Like everything her mother chose, it was both pretty and practical. She was beginning to miss her mother.

When Lucy came back from the bathroom Darci had turned off the light over her bed.

"Let's get some sleep." she said. "I've got to look good for my big scene tomorrow." Her voice was cool and affected. "Forget all that silly stuff, Lucy. I make things up all the time. After all, I've been acting since I was a little girl." She slid down under the bedclothes and shut her eyes.

Lucy studied Darci, who lay in bed without makeup, curled up like a child. She could see their resemblance for the first time, in the shape of Darci's face and her features too. But from what Lucy knew so far, she certainly hoped the likeness wasn't more than skin deep!

The sun was still hidden in mist as Lucy stood at the Oceanbluff pool the next morning. There were at least twenty-five people milling around, but she didn't see any of the cast. The "gaffers," as the lighting electricians were called, set up reflectors and ran cable along one side of the pool. A camera assistant was opening up a small wooden tripod. Ross Rubell, the Director of Photography, stood beside him.

"Hi," Priscilla greeted Lucy, "want a second breakfast?" She was wearing a stopwatch around her neck and holding a clipboard.

"Sure." Lucy followed Priscilla to a long table set up behind the pool cabanas. Next to the large urns of coffee and hot water were trays of Danish pastry, burritos, fruit, and other food. This is California, all right, Lucy thought. Who'd ever heard of burritos at this hour?

"I need tanks of coffee to get myself started," Priscilla said, reaching for a plastic cup.

With her huge innocent eyes and her wispy hair, Priscilla looked as though she was out to lunch half the time. But Lynne said she was one of the best script supervisors in town. That meant not only keeping careful track of every word in the script, but of the details of costume and action too.

"So how was Darci this morning?" Priscilla asked.

"We hardly talked. She was stewing over her lines but otherwise she seemed fine."

"Can you believe it? Her mother's here already. In fact she was here with her husband when I arrived with the crew."

Lucy looked around for Mavis Toone.

"She's probably in Darci's dressing room, driving

her crazy." Priscilla went on, pointing to the long line of trailers and trucks in the roadway.

"I've been wondering about the cast. No one seems to be around."

"They usually stay in their dressing rooms until they're called. No one but the crew steps on the actual set until the director says so."

Priscilla put down her cup. "I'd better go, before Van starts yelling. He wants me right next to him every second."

"See you later." Lucy had one eye on Lynne's blue BMW, pulling to a stop beside the prop truck. Lynne stepped out of her car and headed toward the breakfast table with her easy, long-legged walk. Her tall slim figure was spectacular in white slacks and a rust-colored cotton sweater.

"Hello, Lucy." Lynne called. As she reached the table, she added, "What kind of shape is Darci in this morning?"

"Hi, Lynne. She's fine, I guess."

"That's not quite convincing."

"I was going to say, she certainly dramatizes herself a lot, doesn't she."

"And how. Trying to bring back the days of her former glory." Lynne reached for a cup of coffee. "Where's your father?"

"Dad drove us over, but then he left for a meeting."

"Oh, right. He'll be at Lorcaster all morning. That's the big production company that's backing our series." She looked at her watch. "I'd better go say good morning to my cast. I hope you don't get too bored. You know by now that shooting a TV show is more standing around and waiting than anything else. Oh, and don't forget that Timon's expecting you at nine. Walk back down here when you're finished and we'll pick you up for lunch."

"Okay. See you."

When Lucy got back to the pool, the tempo was speeding up. "I'm going to go put a mike on Slade," the sound man called out to Van. Across the pool, Priscilla was right at Van's elbow.

Suddenly Priscilla seemed to trip on the cable. Van's hand went out to her but it was too late. There was a shout and a loud splash.

"Come *on,* Priscilla!" Van wailed.

"Can she swim?" someone asked above the laughter of the crew.

"All California kids can swim," someone else answered.

Lucy rushed to the edge of the pool and saw Priscilla splashing around in the water. Was she bobbing up and down to cover her embarrassment?

"What's the matter, Priscilla?" Ross called out.

"Are you okay?" Lucy found herself shouting.

Priscilla made feeble efforts to tread water. Choking and spitting, she was unable to talk.

Suddenly the assistant cameraman, Angelo, pulled off his shirt and jumped into the water. He struggled to grab hold of Priscilla and managed to bring her to the side of the pool. As several of the crew reached for Priscilla, Angelo began to spit and cough too.

Now there were voices on all sides: "Say, Angelo, what's with you?" "Get something to wrap her in! Beach towels, anything!"

37

Lynne's voice surfaced over the confusion. She called to the production manager, "Don't let anyone near the pool. I'll send for an ambulance."

Several of the men carried Priscilla to a lounge chair, as others helped Angelo. He sat on the concrete pool apron with his head on his knees. By now a crowd of new faces had gathered from the wardrobe and makeup trailers and the sound and prop trucks.

Darci trotted down the lawn with Mark close behind her and peered into the pool. Slade was already walking straight around the pool to Priscilla. Lucy hurried behind her.

"I'm sure someone's called an ambulance," Slade said as she bent over Priscilla and felt her head. "What happened, Van?"

"She tripped and fell into the pool."

"And Angelo?"

"He fished her out."

"Watch the cable," Ross shouted as Lucy followed Slade to the edge of the pool.

"The water looks perfectly fine," Slade said, "and there's no peculiar smell."

Lynne strode back to the pool beside a man in a blue blazer with a gold club insignia. Lucy guessed he was the manager.

"We'll take some water samples, then we'll empty the pool," the man said to Lynne.

An ambulance wailed in the distance.

Lucy looked back at Priscilla. She was clutching her stomach. The next moment she passed out.

Yesterday, Darci—today, Priscilla! Was there a connection? What was going on?

Chapter Four

After the ambulance drove off, Lucy flopped into a chair beside the pool wishing there was someone to talk to. Everyone had scattered once the hour "break" was announced. Would Priscilla be all right? How much delay would there really be, and how much trouble would it cause? Had her father learned about it yet?

The pool water was already noticeably lower when two Oceanbluff employees began to take samples. What could be in the water anyway? Probably someone had used too free a hand with a chemical meant to disinfect the pool. Surely it had been a mistake. Otherwise—

A scraping sound broke into Lucy's thoughts. Slade was tugging at a heavy lounge chair and Mark was trying to help her.

"I'll tell you what you *can* do for me, Mark," Slade said. "There must still be some hot water on the table. Be a good fellow and get me some tea. And how about you, Lucy?"

"No, thank you," Lucy murmured, startled at being included.

Slade made herself comfortable in the lounge chair

and watched Mark walk off. An electric-blue terry cloth robe emphasized her eyes.

"Beautiful young man," she said slowly. "Hollywood children don't always turn out that way."

Lucy played with a fingernail. "I don't know him very well yet."

"You'll see. He's grown up with a famous father, a mother who's a power at the studios, and everything money can buy. But he doesn't lean on any of it."

Slade stared at the pool. "I'm puzzled about Priscilla. She's a bit fey, but as good a continuity girl as I've ever known. The pupils of her eyes were just pinpoints, and that may have something to do with what happened. Could she have taken some drug?"

"I don't think so Sla—uh, Ms. . . ."

"Slade will do."

"Thanks. I was going to say that Priscilla and I had coffee together just a little while ago. She was absolutely okay then. I even noticed her eyes, and they looked perfectly normal."

"How long was she in the water?"

"About three or four minutes."

"When my dresser told me what happened, I came down as I was, ready for my scene."

Of course. Lucy remembered the script. The pool scene opened as Slade took off a beach robe and walked down the graded steps at the shallow end of the pool. Though over sixty, the domineering head of the Martin family swam a half mile each morning. This particular morning, her grandson was to confront her at the club about a business decision she'd made. Was Darci in the scene too? Yes, Lucy remembered, but later. First Mark followed Slade into the pool to continue the argument. Darci was supposed to find them there.

"You're miles away, Lucy," Mark said as he handed Slade her tea. "Are you okay?"

"Sure. I was thinking about this morning. If Priscilla hadn't tripped, Slade would have been the first person in the pool."

"Did you think of that, Menacing Mother?" Mark asked Slade as he hauled over a chair.

"Listen, Son of Satan, it could have been you. The way Van keeps changing the action, you might have led the parade."

"And Darci?" Lucy said. "What about her?"

"She doesn't show up until we're pages into the scene. There's no way that would play."

"Then whatever's in the pool was put there for one of you!" Lucy caught her breath. She hadn't meant to be so blunt.

"Don't get carried away, Lucy," Slade said calmly. "This wasn't a deliberate act. Just some unfortunate carelessness with the chemicals they use. But in any case, that little Priscilla probably went off in the ambulance instead of me. I feel sorry for the poor girl." Slade stood up. "I think I'll rest in my dressing room for a while."

As Slade walked off, Lucy was left alone with Mark, who had been silent beside them. Lucy had nothing to say to him. Maybe she'd overreacted during the chase scene the day before, but she wasn't ready to forget it.

"I'm going to go up to the barn," Lucy said. "Maybe Timon can work with me early."

"I'll walk you up there." Mark got out of his chair. They walked out to the road and headed for the stable.

"I'd like to explain about yesterday," Mark said finally.

"It doesn't matter," Lucy said. "Everything turned out all right."

"And how. You really put yourself into the scene."

"Did I have any choice?"

"That's what I wanted to talk about. You were so riled up at the time, there wasn't much point."

Lucy took long strides and looked straight ahead.

"Maybe I went too far," Mark continued, "but I was trying to force you to play the scene. Even in a long shot, the audience knows if you're just going through the motions."

"Does that mean I have to go down the ravine?"

"Of course not. But you took this on. You said your father thought you'd have fun, but from what I know of him, he thought you'd do what was necessary too. I wanted you to feel what it was like to get into the part and really mean it. I would have backed off before anything went wrong."

"I'd never have guessed that from the look on your face."

"I was acting, Lucy."

"And you like to act, don't you."

"Not particularly. I fell into it when a friend of my dad's thought I looked just right for a part in his picture. I'm going back to UCLA next fall. Then I'll get back to archeology. That's what I really go for."

"That's a surprise."

"I've already spent three different summers on

42

archeological digs. You really don't know me very well."

Embarrassed, Lucy looked off at a row of metal stalls at the edge of the road.

"This is where we do our easy scene," Mark said. "The one where we walk together while you put Durkin away."

"I'd forgotten about that. What a beautiful chestnut over there, look!" Lucy walked up to the stalls with Mark beside her. "He reminds me of Moonrock, my teacher's horse in Connecticut. They could be twins."

As Lucy talked to the horse, he allowed her to stroke his nose. The longing for Up and Down Farm made her chest ache. She'd been back there only once in the six months she'd lived in New York. She felt the soft muzzle under her hand. Standing there looking at the Pacific and thinking of Connecticut made her feel she was nowhere at all.

"Are we friends again?" Mark said quietly at her shoulder.

"We'll just start over."

"Fine. Can I watch your lesson—I mean, may I?"

Lucy turned to him in surprise. "How come you said that?"

"Because 'can I' isn't good grammar."

"I know, but how come you correct yourself like that?"

"Rita's a writer and a story editor, remember? From the moment I could talk she's been after me about may and can—"

"Take and bring, who and whom, yeah and yes. My mother reminds me all the time."

Mark smiled. "I recognize a fellow sufferer. See, we have to be friends."

It was a relief to get back to Van's, Lucy thought as she relaxed in a chair on the sun deck. After her lesson with Timon she'd had nothing to do all afternoon but watch everyone else work. She hadn't seen her father until they'd "wrapped" for the day.

Right now he was playing Ping-Pong with Van at the corner of the deck. Lynne came out to the deck and sank into a chair. She shook down the ice cubes in the tall glass in her hand. "Some days are worse than others," she said.

Lucy sat up. "How's Priscilla? Do they know what was in the pool?"

"She's going to be fine. The doctor explained it to me. There was an insecticide in the water—one that contains an organophosphorus compound. That whole group of insecticides is absorbed through the skin very quickly, and of course, Priscilla swallowed plenty too. The narrow pupils, the sweating, the nausea—they're all standard symptoms."

"Do they use that kind of stuff at Oceanbluff?" Lucy asked.

"Yes, in weak concentrations. The insecticide's called Luthathione. It comes in large bags, and they dissolve it in water to spray on the trees. The grounds-people wear protective gear when they use it. Fortunately, the amount in the pool was just enough to cause trouble, but not enough to be lethal.

"The club manager asked all the employees to check the grounds for empty Luthathione sacks, and they

44

found several in a garbage pail not far from the pool. None of the employees had mixed any for a while."

"Where do they usually keep the sacks?" Mr. Hill stood at the Ping-Pong table drinking from a glass he had parked nearby.

"In a shed that's nowhere near the pool."

"And it's usually locked?"

"That's what they say."

Mr. Hill twirled the Ping-Pong paddle still in his hand. "Would you like a game, Lucy?"

"Maybe later, Dad."

Van paced back and forth. "Could one of the hired hands have pulled some kind of a sick joke?"

Lynne shook her head. "That's what I wondered, but the manager says all his people have worked at the club at least five years. He trusts them. And anyone can buy Luthathione in a garden supply store or even in a large supermarket."

"Will Priscilla be in the hospital long?" Lucy asked.

"Three or four days. Luckily, they know exactly how to reverse the reaction to Luthathione with a drug called atropine. If she hadn't developed some trouble with her lungs, she'd probably go home tomorrow, like Angelo."

"Will she come back to the shoot?"

"We'll see," Lynne said. "The new woman the union sent out is really very good. Priscilla will probably rest up and go to a new production. Don't worry, Lucy. She always gets work."

"I really like her. Besides, she promised to show me a videotape of *The Little Soldier*."

Mr. Hill turned from the sunset which had striped

the sky with orange and rose. "Darci's films have never been released on video cassette." He slapped Van on the back and dropped into a canvas chair. "Ask Van. He'd love to make the extra money. Anyway, someone should be very grateful to Priscilla. She took a Luthathione bath for *someone.*"

"It had to be Mark or Slade, right Dad? They would have been the first ones in the pool?"

"I guess so." Her father sounded angry. "Unfortunately, I'm the real target here. People are in danger because of me."

"You? But you weren't even there!"

"I'm talking about my schedule and my reputation. If anything happens to one of my stars—"

"Now we're all getting the same vibes," Van said, perching on the deck railing. He and Mr. Hill exchanged a look.

"Jake?" Lynne said.

"That guy," Van said, "lives back in one of the canyons and he knows his way over every foot of Malibu. He could easily have found a way into the club at night."

Lucy began to catch on. They were talking about the special-effects guy, Jake. Hadn't he left the union hearing threatening to "get" her father?

"Do you think we need some security, Allan?" Van asked.

"I hate to make everyone work in that kind of atmosphere." He shrugged. "But why kid myself? When Lorcaster hears about this, we'll have security people shoulder to shoulder whether we like it or not."

Lucy drifted away from the conversation. The car

bomb and now the pool. Who knew what Jake would pull next. Her father must be wondering too. But suppose Darci had been right about someone fooling around with her drink? Jake certainly wasn't responsible for that!

A number of intriguing questions had turned up in the last few days. Maybe she should look for some of the answers. It would give her more to do, and she just might head off some trouble for her father. After all, she'd solved two mysteries already, one at Mr. Kendrick's stable in Connecticut and one in New York at Parkside Stable.

"What scenes are you shooting tomorrow, Dad?"

"We'll keep the week's schedule in place and redo the pool scene in overtime Saturday morning."

"So we'll stay up here an extra night?"

"It looks that way."

"Could Darci stay overnight again tomorrow?" Lucy ignored their surprise.

"It's fine with me, Lucy," Van said. "Why don't you ask her. All the personnel numbers are by the phone."

"Thanks, Van. I will."

Lucy went to the living room. But instead of calling Darci, she began to make a list on the pad next to the phone:

Why did Darci think someone spiked her drink? Is she afraid of someone?

What did Darci's mother mean when she said "You can't tell me off for six more months"?

What was wrong between Timon and Mark?

Timon had really been rude to Mark, always using his last name, barking instructions, never saying a single unnecessary word.

When Lucy had finished writing, she phoned Darci and found her at home.

"Hello, Darci. It's Lucy, Lucy Hill."

"Oh, hello."

"I watched both your scenes this afternoon. You were really good."

"Yeah—well, thanks."

"I wondered if you'd like to stay over here again tomorrow night. I know it's closer to the set and, well, we could swim and—"

"Sure, Lucy." Darci actually sounded eager.

"We could watch some of Van's old movies on the VCR. He's got a huge collection."

"I'd like that a lot."

"So I'll expect you, okay? Come straight from the shoot."

"It's a deal."

Lucy felt peculiar when she hung up. Darci had seemed so happy to come that she felt ashamed of her ulterior motives.

Mr. Hill came into the room. "You were going to call your mother tonight. I think you'd better do it now. Don't forget, it's three hours later in New York."

"Thanks, Dad."

"There's a phone in my room, if you want privacy."

"This is okay. We don't have any secrets from you." She picked up the phone and pushed the tiny squares that made up her mother's number. Her hand tightened on the receiver.

"Mom? Hi! How are you?"

"Just fine, Lucy. Fine. And you? Are you having a good time?"

"Sure. Great!"

"You don't sound so great. Is your father nearby?"

"More or less. We're staying at Van Fortune's house in Malibu. You know, he's the director."

"I didn't know."

"Oh. I guess not. Anyway, there are some people here."

"I suppose your father is showing you a big time in Hollywood."

"Mom, that's silly. Besides, I hardly see him. He's awfully busy."

"I thought that was the point of your visit, to spend some time with your father."

Without thinking, Lucy held the receiver away from her ear. No, she realized, that wouldn't change anything.

"Mom, I'm very glad I came out here. It's fun and its different in a lot of interesting ways." She took a deep breath. "But I miss you. That's why I called."

There was silence at the other end of the phone. "Let's start again, Lucy. I'm sorry. Things are fine here, really. I've a new magazine assignment for *Vacation Vogue*. If these pieces continue, perhaps I can take you along someday. On a really exciting assignment, for instance, Ireland."

"Oh, Mom!"

"We might get to the Dublin Horse Show. Have you done any of your riding scenes yet?"

"Just rehearsals. If I don't get to the Maclay, I might become a stunt rider. Who knows."

"You'll be careful."

"Of course."

"It's very quiet here. No calls from Allison or Debby."

"Have you heard from Eric?"

"Last night. He had some kind of a big brother message about not pulling any of your old *stunts.*" They both laughed.

There was a long pause. "Lucy, I don't want to call you there. But call me again. I miss you. More than you know."

As Lucy hung up the phone she burst into tears. Her mother almost never came right out and said things like that. Suddenly, Lucy wanted to be back in New York with her mother's classical records playing in the background and the typewriter clacking away. But of course she wanted to be here too. She'd been having a great time, and the best was still ahead. Her father was trying to show her he loved her every way he could. And right now, he needed her too. Why did her parents have to break up anyway, and start her running east and west, so she didn't even know where she wanted to be? What she needed was one fixed place at the center of her life.

Lucy heard Lynne's soft laughter from the deck. A wave of anger made her clench her fists. Why should her mom be alone in New York when Lynne was having a good time with her father out here? She wasn't going back out to the deck no matter what. She'd go get an apple from the kitchen and then walk on the beach. What had happened to Lynne's cameraman husband, anyway? With fierce strokes of her pen, Lucy added that question to her list.

Chapter Five

"Lucy?"

As she opened her eyes to the early morning, Lucy was surprised to hear her father's voice at the door. The clock said 5:30. They'd agreed the night before that she wouldn't go to the morning's shoot.

"Hi, Dad. Come in." Lucy stretched hard and sat up in bed. "Change of plans?"

"Yes and no. We're still going to work at Pepperdine University down the road. But Van thinks we can finish up early and come back for two scenes at the stables. We'll do the scene with Mark and Slade and the one with Mark and Darci. That means you, too."

Lucy felt her stomach flutter. "You mean the scene where Mark walks with me and I put Durkin back in his stall?"

"Yes. So do whatever you were going to this morning, then have some lunch at the clubhouse and show up at the makeup truck around two thirty. Got that? Two thirty."

Lucy rubbed her eyes and looked closely at her father. "You seem tired. I guess these hours get to you after a while."

"It's not the hours, it's the aggravation." He pushed

his black hair off his forehead. "Truth is, there's nothing I like to do more. Not that *Malibu* is my idea of great art. You've heard your mother take off on that. But it's decent entertainment and it's giving me a chance to build a track record out here."

"You'll make all kinds of terrific shows before you get through. I know it."

Her father came over to the bed and gave Lucy a quick hug. "We'll see. I just want to turn out this show for a while without all the drama on the sidelines. So far no one's been hurt, but we've come much too close."

"But none of it's your fault!"

"That's true, but it's not going to do me any good to be known as the accident-prone producer." Mr. Hill sat down on the edge of the bed. "Lorcaster could even take me off the production if things go on like this."

Lucy moved closer to her father. "Maybe the union will agree that Jake was at fault. Then everyone in Hollywood will know what really happened."

"I'm sure of it. The union will discipline Jake and he won't work again for years. But he'll try to get even."

Lucy had never seen her father's eyes look so troubled. "I wish I was older. Then I could work with you. Maybe do Lynne's job, and really help."

"It's a help just to talk to you, Lucy." He hugged her. "I love you very much and it makes me feel good to have a daughter like you."

Lucy was speechless. That was the biggest compliment her father had ever given her. Last night her mother, now her father!

"I guess since I'm getting older, we can really be friends."

"I'm counting on it." Her father stood up decisively. "Well, honey, you're sure you don't want to change your mind and come along?"

"Yes, Dad. I might watch an old movie on the VCR, if that's okay. After that I'll go up to the stable and see if I can pick up a ride."

"Fine. Only don't get tired out," he said, with exaggerated seriousness. "You're making your screen debut today."

"Sure, Dad. With my back to the camera." They laughed together.

As the door closed behind her father the flutter in Lucy's stomach came back. More than ever, she wanted her three scenes to be perfect. Her father had taken a big chance so that she could do something special during this vacation. Putting the horse away shouldn't be any trouble—the chase scene either. But the rear and fall was another story. She'd have to work even harder to get it right by Monday.

Right now Lucy had something else on her mind— last night's list of questions. She'd get some of the answers from Darci at the end of the day. This morning she'd start with Timon.

When Lucy arrived at the stable toward the end of the morning, Timon was walking Durkin at the far end of the ring. As he sat in the saddle, there was certainly nothing elegant about his big, powerful body, but still he looked as though he belonged on a horse.

"Hello!" Lucy called. "You teaching Durkin some new tricks?"

Timon shook his head as he trotted toward her. "Just wearing him out a little so he'll be easier to handle tomorrow. Was I supposed to work with you?"

"No. I thought I'd hang out around the barns and try to fix up a ride."

"You can ride Durkin, if you want." Timon stopped in front of her. "I'll get Moolah, my Quarter Horse."

"That would be great. I don't suppose I could pop a few fences?" Lucy looked longingly at the two rows of jumps in the center of the ring.

"Not today." He slid off Durkin and handed Lucy the reins. "Just let him limber up. I'll be right back."

Lucy hoisted herself into the saddle and adjusted the stirrups. Walking along the ring rail, she was caught up in the beauty of the day. Wispy clouds looked like lint on the pale blue sky. The ocean was calm, with just a few fringes of white. Lucy worked at a posting trot, then collected the horse for a sitting trot. Relaxing into the familiar routine, she realized just how keyed up she'd been for the last few days. All the new people and impressions had been a big stretch.

It was reassuring to give the horse the familiar leg signals and get the right response, to make contact with his mouth and know her hands were light and capable. Once again she looked toward the fences in the center of the ring. She'd better get back to regular training soon, or she'd never make it to the National Horse Show.

Timon rode back toward the ring on a smallish brown horse with a broad chest and sturdy legs. The ungainly man appeared larger than ever on the stocky little animal, but somehow the two seemed to suit one another. Lucy stared at the saddle. A striped Mexican blanket was folded underneath it, but the whole thing was much lighter than the tooled leather saddles, ornate with silver, that Lucy thought of as western. The pommel was smaller too.

Lucy fell in love with Moolah on sight. Though he carried his head low, like western horses, you could tell he had a jaunty personality. He seemed happy just to be out in the air with a rider on his back.

Timon opened and closed the ring gate from the horse's back.

"He's adorable, Timon! How old is he?"

"Four and a half."

Lucy studied Moolah's halterlike bridle. A leather noseband reached around under his chin, the reins attached to the ends. A second leather band circled the underside of his jaw. But there was no bit in his mouth at all!

"I've never seen a bridle like that," Lucy said, moving up to walk beside Timon. "How do you control him?"

"I'm using a hackamore—or a *jaquima,* as they say out here. It presses against the sensitive parts of the nose and the jaw. Most western horses work a long time without a bit because otherwise, the training's too hard on their mouths. They have to learn to stop on a dime from a fast gallop and to make sudden sharp turns off their haunches. After Moolah learns the basics, I'll train him to the bit. Then later, he'll answer just to reins against his neck and the way I shift my weight in the saddle."

"When will he be ready for the movies and TV work?"

Timon snorted. "I've got bigger plans for this guy. He's my chance for the real bucks! I suppose you've never been to a horse show with western or stock horse classes. Well, some of that prize money makes Grand Prix jumping stakes look like change for the Laundromat. I'm going to show Moolah," Timon said, "or sell him. Plenty of kids around here as anxious to win the Stock Seat Equitation Championship as you are to take home the Maclay."

"I had no idea. I never paid any attention to western riding. I—"

"Of course not. A lot of you eastern riders are snobs. So are some of our riders out here. Mark Ladd's been riding since he was three and I bet he's never been in a western saddle."

There's your opening, Lucy thought. Only she was too interested in what Timon was saying to change the subject. He was certainly much more willing to talk when he wasn't giving a lesson. And when Mark wasn't around.

"But Durkin is trained just like any horse back home. You ride hunt seat, too, right?"

"Of course. I train all kinds of horses for all kinds of scenes."

"Is that why your saddle looks so strange? It's sort of a cross between English and western."

"You don't need the high pommel if you're not carrying a rope. And we've taken some pointers from your hunt seat—this saddle gets your weight forward and puts your legs right under you."

"I wish I could take some extra lessons with you," Lucy said fervently. "You could teach me a lot more than—"

"You thought?"

Lucy blushed. "No! I didn't mean . . ." She trailed off lamely.

"Let's get to work," Timon said.

Lucy swallowed hard and reached for any question that might continue the conversation.

"How did you get started with horses?"

"My pop was an electrician at the film studios," he said. "When I was about nine there wasn't much work, so he was moonlighting up here in Malibu for some of the rich Hollywood people in the Colony. Well, that year he had a job at Mr. Kirk Ladd's, and he took me with him. My eyes were falling out, I'd never been in a house like that. But what got to me most was this little kid sitting on a pony down on the beach, as though he owned the world. I'd been wanting a horse so badly I'd been losing sleep. And here was the most beautiful pony I'd ever seen, belonging to this kid who wasn't even old enough to know anything."

"You're talking about Mark? Mark Ladd?"

"Who else. I guess I was kind of quiet on the way home and my father finally got out of me what was the matter. He wasn't going to let me get away with feeling sorry for myself. He said if I really wanted to ride,

I could work on one of the ranches up here and learn something.

"So that's how I got started, and now Mark Ladd is on one of my shoots." His voice changed. "And instead of a pony, he's riding a Porsche."

Timon looked around uncomfortably, as though he'd just realized that he'd been talking out loud. "I'm sure you didn't come up here to shoot the breeze. I'm going to put Moolah through some figure eights." He loped off without another word.

Lucy looked after him. He was *still* jealous of Mark. Had he been jealous enough to poison the pool?

In her rush to be on time, Lucy reached the makeup trailer ten minutes early. Slade was already standing there, glancing at her watch beside the locked door. A vivid blue shirt matched her eyes and a dramatic silver necklace, the kind made by American Indians, gleamed against her chest. She stood with her back absolutely straight and her head held high, almost as though she expected to be admired.

"Good afternoon, Lucy. Isn't it a beautiful day?"

"I'll say. It's hard to believe they're having a big blizzard back home."

"As you see, there's no one here. Why don't we go to my dressing room until they come back from Pepperdine."

"Well—thanks, Slade. Really, I . . ." Start again, Lucy, she told herself. Slade won't bite. "Thanks, Slade. That would be neat."

Lucy followed Slade to the lead trailer. When they stepped inside, she was amazed. This "dressing room"

59

was more like an expensive hotel suite on wheels. She tried not to gawk as Slade led her from the living room to the dressing area and bedroom, the kitchen and bath. Then they sat down on a soft overstuffed couch bigger than the one in Lucy's living room at home. As they sipped the iced tea Slade brought from the bar refrigerator, Lucy leaned back against the pillows.

"I watched two of your old films at Van's this morning," Lucy said. "You know, on his VCR."

"Oh? Which ones?"

"Foolish Victory and, um . . . the one with *bridge* in the name."

"That old clinker? *Bridge of Light.* You know, I didn't write them, honey. I just learned my lines."

"It *was* soupy, but I liked it. What was your favorite film you ever made? Van has a wall full of tapes."

"A real oldie, *Days of Dread.* But you won't find it at Van's. It hasn't been distributed on video cassette." Anger tightened Slade's face. "That's not to say hundreds of copies aren't whirring around on VCRs in Brazil, England, the Mideast—"

"How do they get there?"

"It makes me furious. The video pirates get hold of a print somehow and throw thousands of illegal copies on the market." Slade leaned back against the couch. "Anyway, *Days of Dread* was no one else's favorite but mine. I doubt even the pirates want it."

"Did you ever make a picture with Darci?"

"Just once."

They were both silent. Finally Slade spoke. "She was actually an enchanting child, but damaged by her mother's ambition. Poor Darci. I don't think anyone—"

There was a loud knock on the trailer door and Guy, the makeup man, burst into the room. "Sorry about the late start, Miss Porter, but we need you right away. It was a circus this morning, and Van's ready to feed everyone to the lions."

As Slade stood up to go, Guy added, "You come, too, Miss Hill. Rick wants to work on your hairpiece some more before your scene."

Lucy walked at Slade's elbow as they headed for the makeup trailer. Slade was lost in thought.

"Poor Darci. I don't think anyone's ever loved her just for herself, not even Mavis. Her mother was a B player. You're too young to even know what that was, but B films were low-budget flicks the studios cranked out, before television."

Inside the trailer, Lucy followed Slade to a dressing table at the far end. Guy and Rick scurried around unpacking some of their equipment from the kits they'd carried to the morning shoot. Guy laid out jars and pencils in front of Slade as she went on.

"Mavis saw a chance to create a new Shirley Temple with her darling daughter, and I'll hand it to her, she came close. The child was cute as a button. She had some of her father's talent. Then they lucked into Van and he really knew how to direct her."

"Excuse me, Miss Porter," Guy said. "May I start now?"

"Of course. We're just gossiping."

"Lucy, I need you over here," Rick said. He led her to his chair at the other end of the trailer.

"She does look like a younger Darci, doesn't she?" Slade called over to Rick.

The hairdresser began to comb out a fall of long brown hair on a wig stand nearby. "She'll look even more like her when we get the hair right."

"Won't I be wearing a hunt cap?"

"Yes, it's over there with the rest of your clothes. You'll wear this fall in a ponytail. Even from a distance, the two of you have to match exactly."

"Do I have to wear makeup? My back's to the camera!"

"You're the first girl I've met who didn't like makeup."

"I'm just not used to it."

"Perhaps you'll get to like it. You can argue with Guy when you're dressed. You've got at least another hour."

As Rick pinned up her hair, Lucy was torn between watching herself in the mirror and keeping an eye on Slade's progress. She wanted to hear more about Darci as soon as she was free to talk. As Guy worked on Slade's face, Lucy wondered how many hundreds of times—maybe thousands—Slade had been made up for a part. And still she was such a real and natural person underneath. You must have to be very strong to keep from being confused by all those parts. And by all the attention, for that matter.

At last Guy dusted Slade's face with a large powder puff and stood back to view the result. Lucy spoke up quickly.

"Slade, Lynne told me Darci hadn't worked in a long time. Do you know how she got her part in

Malibu? Did it have anything to do with looking like me? That's what Lynne thinks."

"Possibly. But not until she had a chance to see your father. Darci's been trying to get work again for a long time. Either Mavis or Darci must have worked on Van. For old times' sake, you know. Van's career took an awful dip for a while, too, so he knows how it feels. He's only made it back the last few years. And in the beginning Darci was only going to do one or two shows, so it wasn't a very big favor."

A production assistant appeared at the trailer door. "The car's outside to drive you to the location, Miss Porter."

"Fine. Thank you."

A wardrobe woman rushed into the trailer. "Let me check your shirt, Miss Porter. The script supervisor says your necklace was *under* your collar yesterday in the scene before this one. Let me just adjust it. There."

Slade stood up and leaned over the dressing table to look at herself in the mirror. She stroked a finger across one eyebrow and wet her lips. As she passed by Lucy's chair, she patted her shoulder. "I'll come to see your debut later."

Lucy smiled and watched Slade leave the trailer.

"She's the best," Rick said.

"For sure!" Lucy said fervently.

Lucy stood by the metal paddock at the end of the row of stalls where she'd stopped with Mark the day before. She ran her hand under the ponytail that hung down her back and straightened her hunt cap.

"Sorry, Darci," one of the gaffers said, trying to place a booster light where she was standing.

For a second Lucy was puzzled. Then she stepped aside. "I'm Lucy. It's terrific that you were fooled."

Van came up to Lucy and put an arm around her shoulders. "Lucy, pet, this is your breakthrough moment. And here's Mark at last, so we can walk through the scene from the top."

"Hi, guys," Mark said. "Van, do you want me to wear sunglasses or not?"

"Wear them. Now listen hard. If you do this in one take I'll mint a medal for each of you. You'd think film was confetti the way we're using it today."

Van led the way up the road. "Give me a mark here," he yelled and one of the crew came running with yellow chalk.

"You'll start here and walk to the paddock side by side. Lucy will be leading the horse—that is, if Timon ever gets here with him. Mark, you walk beside her and open the gate."

Out of the corner of her eye, Lucy saw Slade arrive and sit down in a folding chair not far from the camera.

"Has the electric fencing been turned off?" Mark asked.

Lucy noted the tiny wire that ran on plastic insulators along the top of the pen.

"I turned it off, Van," one of the gaffers answered.

"Check again."

The electrician walked behind the pen to a red box on a metal post. "It's okay."

Van put a hand to his forehead like a sailor looking

out to sea. "What do I spy? Timon is finally ambling down here with the horse. Ross," he called, "stand by for camera rehearsal."

Everyone stood in uncomfortable silence until Timon arrived. "All right, kiddies," Van snapped. "No time to talk. Lucy, take the horse and show me how you're going to put him away. Mark, walk beside her the way I told you."

As Lucy started forward, her feet felt like two balloons about to take off in the wind. Leading a horse, normally as easy as putting on socks, was suddenly as terrifying as the first trip to the beginners' ring at Up and Down Farm. What was that glass eye in the camera doing to her? She was making Mark awkward too.

"Aw, kiddies, give me a break," Van exploded. "Walk as though you mean it. Nice deliberate steps as if you'd had your vitamins this morning." He pushed them aside and took long strides toward the paddock. "Mark, come right at the gate, like this. Put your hand on it and—"

The next sound was a yelp as Van fell to the road. Mark raced over and knelt beside him. "Hey, Van. Van, what happened? Are you all right?"

Lucy tugged Durkin along with her. Van lay sprawled on the ground and the muscles at the top of his arm were twitching. As Timon took the horse, she looked around in confusion. How could Van have been shocked if the electricity was off?

Now Slade and several of the men in the crew crowded around Van. As Slade felt for a pulse, Van sat up abruptly and waved her away. Lucy followed every step as the men helped him over to his folding chair.

Meanwhile, Mark and a gaffer dashed behind the paddock. First they examined the red box. Then they seemed to be following a wire over to the lowest rail of the paddock. As Lucy craned her neck, they moved back into the low bushes behind the row of stalls.

"I don't know yet how far the wire runs," the electrician yelled, "but the fence is rigged to a different battery altogether."

Mark came running back and explained. "We found a car battery buried in the dirt about a hundred yards away. Someone must have been hiding in the bushes, waiting for the right moment to turn on the current."

Lucy felt her stomach tighten. Another attack against the *Malibu* production, just one day after the pool incident. How would her father feel *now?*

"Come on, Lucy," Mark said. "Van's going home and Ross is going to shoot the scene the way Van blocked it."

"Let's run through the action again," Ross shouted.

Timon brought Durkin to Lucy and they shot the scene. Lucy didn't think about being nervous. She had too much else on her mind.

Chapter Six

Back at the house, Lucy, Lynne, and Darci all pitched in to put together a dinner from the party leftovers.

"So much for women's lib," Darci said. "Do you really think anything's changed? The men are out on the deck and the women are in the kitchen."

"Oh, well," Lynne said, "Van's been semielectrocuted and Allan's worn out with everyday shock. We can be generous. Lucy, there are sprouts for the salad on the windowsill. Darci, you could peel some avocados."

"Did Van go to bed?" Darci asked. "I didn't see him when I arrived."

"I don't think so. He was sick to his stomach for a while but his doctor checked him out. He wants to have supper with us." Lynne garnished a platter of cold meats with slices of orange. "By the way, I checked with Priscilla today. She'll be leaving the hospital in the morning."

"Jake will have all of us on *Malibu* peering behind every bush," Darci said. "Actually, I'm sorry I missed Van's pratfall this afternoon. It would have been a novelty to see him knocked off balance. But who was meant to get zapped?"

"Mark was supposed to open the gate, if that's what you mean. Van was demonstrating how he wanted it done." Lucy carried the salad bowl over to Lynne. "Is this enough lettuce?"

"Fine. You can take it outside to the table."

But Lucy stood there. "Lynne, there's something I don't get. We moved the paddock scene up a day. Everyone's so sure that Jake rigged up the current. But how would he have known about the change in schedule?"

"All those guys on the crews know each other," Darci answered. "They check their homes all day for messages. Jake could find out all kinds of ways."

Lucy looked to see if Lynne agreed. "I'm surprised anyone on Dad's crew would still be talking to Jake."

"That's unrealistic, Lucy. Some of these men have known each other for years. They work together. They drink together. They stick up for each other. Don't forget, Jake has his own version of how the explosion happened."

Lucy took the salad to the sun deck. There was one person, she thought, who would have known about the schedule change right away. He knew a lot about electricity too. After years of helping his father, a simple wiring job to a different battery would have been a cinch for Timon. He could have done it while everyone was at Pepperdine in the morning. Why had he been late bringing Durkin to the paddock? Had he stopped to turn on the current? The crew had finished setting up by then. He would have expected Mark to hit the gate next.

At dinner it was as if everyone had agreed not to

talk about the afternoon's development. Van sat at the head of the table, somewhat pale despite his heavy tan. He peppered the meal with old Hollywood stories and they teased him about his high-voltage personality.

Later Darci studied the shelves of cassettes endlessly.

"Choose *anything*, Darci." Lucy pleaded. "I'm falling asleep." Finally, they watched *All About Eve*, Marilyn Monroe in the first picture that made her well-known.

While Lucy waited for the tape to rewind, Darci left the room. Later, Lucy heard heated quarreling coming from the kitchen. She stood quietly near the door.

"You're wrong for the part, Darci," Van was saying. "Nothing's going to change that."

Lucy wondered how she could have been so dense. Of course Darci had been glad to spend the night. It gave her a chance to work on Van about the feature!

"You've got to give me the part, Van. You know it. That part will put me back on top."

"Leave it alone, Darci. I've already proven I was a friend. Now drop it."

Poor Van, he'd had problems enough for one day. "Excuse me," Lucy said loudly and walked into the kitchen.

"Oh, hello there, Lucy. Can I help you with anything?"

"Dad and I stowed a tank of apple juice in the fridge. I was going to get a glass."

"Sure, Lucy. Help yourself." Van walked out of the room.

Darci looked after him thoughtfully. She tossed her

head and made a face. "I liked him a lot better when I was little. Let's go for a swim, Lucy, what do you say?"

The ocean was gentle under the moonlight. When Van turned on the spotlights, the bright spill was a jarring intrusion. As she raced down the beach to the water, Darci was startling in a peppermint striped string bikini. Lucy strolled after her in her green and black one-piece suit. Would she ever have a figure worth showing off?

A strong swimmer, Lucy moved comfortably along on the top of the waves as Darci arched and vanished under one crest after another.

"You're a dolphin!" Lucy said, as they finally floated together beyond the breakers.

"Really. Everyone out here has special tanks to dunk in—hot, cold, whirling, twirling. The ocean's my space. Sometimes I think I was a fish in a former life."

Stretched out on her back, Darci was able to chatter easily. Lucy had never been much good at floating that way. As she tried to talk, her face was repeatedly awash.

"Let's go back to the beach," she soon said. "We can talk better."

Darci broke into a crawl and raced the waves back to the sand.

"Hey!" Lucy called after Darci. She was grateful for a few strong waves that helped to carry her back to shore. Darci was already wrapped in a large beach towel and staring at the horizon. Lucy sat down quietly beside her.

"You know what I'd like to do?" Darci said, after a

while. "I'd like to float out on one of those waves as far as it would take me and leave this whole Hollywood rat race forever."

"You can't really mean that! The movies have been your whole life!"

"It seems that way, but I'm not sure Darci Rutland has anything to do with me. No more than Calloway Martin's evil granddaughter, or any other part I've played."

Lucy was astonished. She said nothing, hoping Darci would go on.

"My mother turned me into an actress when I was a kid. I loved all the attention—the fan mail, the parties, the trucks full of toys. You know, absolute strangers knit me so many sweaters, I felt sorry for the sheep. But when things went sour, well, Mavis turned it into my fault. I just had growth hormone in my body like everyone else. But it was the end of the joyride, and she hated me for it."

"Your mother adores you, Darci."

"Don't be a dope. She's an actress. A two-bit actress, but good enough to fawn over me when she thinks it will help. I got Van to give me a chance in this series, so suddenly I'm her darling Darci again. She can talk about early morning calls and right and left profiles—live her life through me."

"But you still want to act, don't you? Why else did you talk Van into giving you a part in *Malibu?* Why are you trying to get a lead in his feature?"

"Sometimes I don't know what I want. Of course I'd like to be back in the spotlight. Who wouldn't? Besides, I don't know if I can do anything else."

"If you're tired of Hollywood, you could give the theater a try. Maybe you should work in New York for a while. You could study somewhere—like at the Actors Studio."

"What for?" Darci's voice was suddenly harsh. "The cameras roll and I act. Look, has your father been saying anything to you? What are you trying to tell me, Lucy? That I'm getting canned?"

"Come off it, Darci. Big stars like Farah Fawcett and Jessica Lange have worked there. You're pretty jumpy, you know."

"Thanks, kid. First I can't act. Now I'm a basket case."

"That's not what I meant. You've got good reason for being nervous. You told me so Tuesday night, remember? You thought someone spiked your drink."

Darci fussed with the strap of her suit. "Oh, that. Well, yeah. But it was silly. Uh, I always get sick on champagne. I didn't want to admit it. Let's go up to the house."

"But, Darci, all sorts of terrible things are happening to Dad's production. And it's all been meant for his stars! If you're in *more* danger, maybe from someone besides Jake—"

Darci had seemed miles away as Lucy talked. Now she cocked her head and looked Lucy in the eye.

"I've decided to tell you. You'll only be around another week or so anyway. But don't go blabbing to a soul. The person I'm afraid of is my stepfather."

"Mr. Toone? He seemed really nice!"

"Don't believe it. When I couldn't get work anymore, my mother decided to feather her nest some

72

other way. I don't know why she picked him. He's not in show business, he's an accountant. They met when she was looking for someone to handle my money, and I think the two of them are taking me to the cleaners."

"You mean they're getting into the money you earned when you were little? How can they do that?"

"Easy. My mother controls all my money. It's in a trust fund until I'm twenty-one and meanwhile she can use whatever she says she needs for my support. Ray got into the act to increase the income, improve the investments and all that. But I never get to see the figures, and I wouldn't understand them anyway."

"Darci, you don't honestly think your mother and Ray would put knockout drops in your drink?"

Darci's eyes widened. "Don't you understand? They want to knock me out for good!" Her face began to tremble.

A large golden retriever came bounding up the beach and jumped on Lucy. Darci paid no attention, completely caught up in her story.

A woman whistled at the ocean's edge and the dog ran off.

"Lucy, don't you see. I'll be twenty-one in six months. Then it's *my* money. They have to get rid of me before that." Darci looked off down the beach. "What a beautiful retriever," she said, as though seeing the dog for the first time.

Lucy turned to Darci with amazement. Evidently she'd played her scene to its end and was back in the real world. From what Lucy had seen Darci did as much acting offscreen as on. But why should she make up a story like that?

"Come on, Lucy, let's have another quick swim. Then I'll race you to the house."

Lucy got to her feet. She'd already learned the easiest thing to do with Darci was just to go along. But she'd been swept along by her story, too, and it seemed as though Darci had counted on that.

Friday afternoon, Lucy and Mark rode their horses idly around the ring, waiting for a signal from the production unit in the hills. The big chase scene was about to be filmed. Lucy was more excited than nervous. Mark was now a friend and Durkin a good partner. She leaned forward over the horse's neck and gave him a hug. He was definitely a candidate for her half dozen favorite horses.

"Let's go, Lucy," Mark called as he moved Haywire toward the ring gate. "We're on."

They started up the mountain trail with a production assistant walking behind them. "We're on our way," he said into his walkie-talkie. It was another incredible day, perfect for riding, for shooting a TV show, for just about anything. Maybe this kind of weather could get boring but she'd like a chance to find out.

The clutter of people and equipment looked incongruous against the sparse desert landscape. Once again, Timon was on a hill above the trail, but this time there was a camera beside him as he pointed out the line of action to Van and Ross. Lucy spotted a second camera on the hill, about fifty feet away.

"Mark, where's Darci?" Lucy said. "Doesn't she have to make the close-ups?"

"She's probably cowering in her dressing room. They're going to drive her up here later and see what they can fake with Durkin and a wind machine. If she'll just sit on his back and lean forward, his mane will blow and make it look as though they're moving."

"You're kidding, aren't you?"

"The machine's over there."

Lucy nodded, distracted, and looked from one clump of people to the other. Her father wasn't there. Maybe he'd been afraid to make her nervous. Or maybe he was so nervous himself that he didn't want to watch.

"All right, kiddies," Van bellowed into his megaphone. "Attention, please. We're going to try hard to get this in one take."

Lucy smiled at Mark. Van's standard opening was getting to be a joke.

"We'll have to walk through it first a number of times for camera position and focus. You understand, Lucy? Timon will give you instructions and I'll break in when I've something to say."

At Timon's orders, Lucy found her old landmarks out of sight of the camera and crew, beyond the fork in the trail. She turned to face the set.

"All right, Lucy, *action*. Start walking this way."

When Lucy walked back toward Timon for the fourth time, she saw her father. Boy, am I glad he got here, she thought. I'd really have been hurt if he missed this!

Van had the megaphone now. "We'll go all out this time. Lucy, back off a few more lengths. Ross says he's picking you up too soon. And come in at a strong walk from the beginning. Got that?"

Lucy waved a salute and cantered back to the fork in the trail. As she waited for her cue, she thought she saw another horse and rider in the distance.

"Okay," Van shouted. "Mean it this time!"

The next time he said, "Give me still more."

The third time he yelled through the megaphone, "You're both great. Just one more rehearsal."

Shooting a TV show is really hard work, Lucy thought, walking Durkin back to the starting position yet again. There were so many things to get right—the light, the camera, the sound, the action. And all at the same time.

Lucy looped her reins over one arm and straightened her hunt cap. What was that sound? Hoofbeats were coming closer, and at a gallop.

"Action," Van called, and Lucy started forward. As she reached the main trail, a heavyset man on a large Appaloosa raced toward her down the other fork. Skillfully, he circled around behind her, like a cowboy cutting out a calf, and whipped Durkin across the rump. Durkin took off in the direction the man had come. Lucy tightened her legs, shortened her reins, and thundered along the unfamiliar trail, every stride taking her farther from the set.

There was no point in shouting. She could sense that the rider behind her was gaining steadily. As the trail moved around the side of the next hill, a deep ravine gaped beside them.

Durkin kicked out hard as the powerful, spotted horse came close against his heels. The horse moved away, but Lucy was dangerously near the edge of the ravine.

Now the rider drew alongside and began to press her off the trail. Instinctively, Lucy pulled back on Durkin with all her strength. The horse knew this routine well. Even before she could give him the signal, Durkin wheeled and raced back toward the set.

"Go, Durkin, go!" Lucy yelled, pounding her legs into her horse's sides. She raised herself in the saddle to a gallop position and gave Durkin his head. Don't look over your shoulder, don't! she told herself. Don't even twitch your eyebrow. Just keep on going until you see people. They'll be out looking for you by now.

Behind her, the hoofbeats seemed to slow down. Don't look. Keep galloping. It could be a trick. But from the sound of the fading footsteps, the Appaloosa was speeding off in the other direction.

Pulling Durkin back to a canter, Lucy turned quickly and watched the big man in the plaid shirt disappear around the hill. Her heart was pounding so hard she could barely think. Could this have been Jake? Had he mistaken her for Darci? Was he trying again to hurt her father?

Lucy was suddenly furious. No one was going to damage her father's reputation this time. There was something she could do. At least, she could if she stopped shaking.

"Lucy? Are you all right?" a voice called from the distance. Timon came into view on the trail ahead. "What happened?" he yelled, running toward her.

Lucy slowed Durkin to a walk. She knew she had the right idea if she could just pull it off.

"I'm fine. I'm really sorry, Timon. Durkin took off with me, that's all." She turned her face away. She always hated to seem stupid.

Of course she'd have to tell her father the truth later. But Lorcaster and the rest of Hollywood didn't have to know. Her thigh muscles trembled. Her heart was still thumping.

Timon reached for Durkin's reins and punished him by jerking on his mouth. Lucy winced. I owe you one, boy, she thought. A big carrot and maybe even a lump of sugar.

Timon looked at Lucy carefully. Did he suspect there was more to her story than she'd told him? After all, he knew Durkin's even temperament better than anyone.

"You're sure you're okay?"

"Of course, Timon. You'll see."

He walked off a short distance, then turned to look at her again. "I'll walk you to your mark."

"Then you can't watch the scene. You'll have to stay out of sight."

"I'll see the dailies tomorrow. Van will okay it."

"Thanks, then." She couldn't be on the defensive when she'd gotten herself into this. To her surprise, walking down the path with Timon steadied her a lot.

Again, he stared at Durkin. "He seems quiet enough now." Lucy shrugged her shoulders.

A production assistant appeared with her walkie-talkie. "Are you ready? Van's decided to shoot it this time."

"All set." Lucy forced a smile.

The intercom crackled. *"Action."* Lucy walked forward.

The scene came alive as the memory of her recent narrow escape heightened every action. She fought Mark off as though her life was really at stake. Finally, Durkin wheeled dramatically and they galloped back toward the start mark at a speed she'd never dared before.

"How did it go?" Timon asked as she reached him and slowed Durkin to a walk.

"I think it was the best yet."

"You didn't have any trouble stopping him this time?"

Lucy bit her lip.

Mark trotted up on Haywire. "Do they need another take for a safety?" Timon asked.

"No. Ross was rolling the time before. They just didn't tell us. That was great, Lucy. We did it. What happened back there?"

"Nothing, really."

"I'm taking Haywire down to the barn. I'll phone you tonight."

"Okay," she said automatically. "I mean, uh, sure."

Lucy's father was walking toward her. She swung off her horse and handed the reins to Timon. "Thanks, Timon."

"That was terrific, honey," her father said, hugging her hard. "Some days I've thought I was crazy to let you do this, but I know my girl."

They started along the trail toward the set. The crew was beginning to wrap for the day. Her father looked so pleased and happy, Lucy hated to ruin his mood.

"Dad," She forced herself to say. "There's something I have to tell you."

Chapter Seven

Lucy sat on Van's couch next to her father. He hugged her protectively and his eyes narrowed with anger as he told Lynne the end of the story.

"Van and I walked the trail later and looked at the hoofprints. That maniac would have run her right off the hill if she hadn't used her head!"

"And you think it was Jake?"

"Dad thought so from the description," Lucy said. "He was heavyset, with brown wavy hair and a square face."

"It certainly sounds like Jake," Lynne said. "He must be off the wall. The pool, the electric gate, and now this! He'll not only be out of the union, he'll land in jail."

"Starting Monday, we'll have guards on the set," Mr. Hill said. "I'll discuss it with Lorcaster tomorrow." He rubbed the back of his neck.

The phone rang. "You get that, honey," he said. "It's probably Mark."

Lucy looked at her father quizzically, then hurried across the room.

"Hello? Hi, Mark. Hold on a minute, will you. I want to get this in the other room."

"How did you know about that, Dad?" she asked on the way to the hall.

"Let Mark tell you."

"Well, hang up for me, okay?"

Once out of sight, Lucy raced for the guest room.

"Okay, Mark. I'm here." She listened for a click from the living room phone.

"You're going back to Benedict Canyon after the pool scene in the morning, right?"

"Right." What was he getting at?

"Well, you're all set for one private lesson at the Equestrian Center with Doreen Ambling."

"You mean the trainer you've been working with?"

"That's the one. I thought we could drive down to L.A. together after lunch."

"That's great, Mark. What will I ride? Do they have school horses over there?"

"Sure. But I thought you'd ride my horse, Ricochet."

Lucy nearly dropped the receiver.

"Your Dad and I arranged it all. I'll have my car at the club. Just be ready to leave with me after the shoot. Okay?"

"More than okay. I don't know how to thank—I mean, well—I'm so happy I can't talk straight."

"Good. I'll see you in the morning."

"Sure, Mark. Thanks again."

She hung up the phone and floated back to the living room. What a terrific guy. Her father wasn't so bad either!

From the bedroom hall, she heard Lynne speaking in a quiet voice. "That was really something—to go ahead and do the scene without telling anyone what happened. Darling, she's quite a girl."

Lucy froze in place. Now wait a minute. Didn't people in Hollywood call everyone darling? No. Not Lynne.

"Lucy, is that you?" her father called from the living room.

"Yes."

She wasn't going to take one step into that room. She wasn't! But how could she stay in the hall forever?

"Are you all right?" her father asked when she finally reached the couch. "You look as though you've been dragged along the ocean floor. Mark's surprise wasn't supposed to—"

"Allan," Lynne said, sending Mr. Hill a piercing look.

Lucy felt as if her face was moving in two directions at once. She turned on Lynne. "What happened to your husband, anyway?"

She saw the shock on her father's face, but Lynne answered calmly. "You heard us talking, didn't you. My husband died three years ago, Lucy, in a sailing accident."

"You and Dad should have told me what was going on. You haven't played fair, and I'm sick of you both!" Lucy turned and ran from the room.

Her father caught up with her in the bedroom hall. "Lucy, Lucy. Honey, calm down." He looked into her eyes. "We're all too tired tonight, but we need to talk about this. We'll do it this weekend. I promise."

He reached out to hug her, but Lucy pulled away.

"There's nothing to talk about. You can do what you want." Tears began to run down her face.

He half smiled. "I haven't seen you lose your temper in a long time. I love you, Lucy."

"Thanks a lot, Dad," she said sarcastically, and closed the door to her room.

Behind the door, Lucy muffled her sobs and listened to her father's footsteps as he walked away. Then she crawled into bed with all her clothes on. She wasn't going to deal with this day one more second. Moments later she was asleep.

"Have you been to the Getty Museum?" Mark asked, pointing at the replica of a Roman villa high above the road.

"No." Lucy checked her boots. She'd polished them to a spectacular shine for her lesson at Mark's stable.

"Well, take a look. The Getty means we're leaving Malibu. Isn't it unreal?"

"Yeah, like a lot of other things out here."

"What's going on, Lucy? Your Dad and I thought we'd come up with a great surprise, but you've been moping around the pool all morning. If you're worried about your lesson, don't be. You'll learn a lot from Doreen, and she's fun."

"It's nothing like that. I've just got to get my head turned around."

"Are you worried about Jake? Are you afraid he'll follow us today?"

"Hey! I hadn't even thought of that."

"Well, I won't let you out of my sight." Mark tossed her his extravagant smile. "We're friends, remember?"

We won't be unless I climb out of this funk, Lucy thought.

"I'm sorry, Mark. The problem is that I've been getting messages about Lynne and my father ever since I arrived out here, but I just closed my mind to them."

"I think Lynne's great."

"I did, too, until . . . Well, it got through to me last night that she and my father are going together or dating or whatever you want to call it."

Mark looked puzzled. "What's wrong with that? Her husband died a few years ago." He paused. "She knew your father back in New York. It seems pretty natural."

"But my father's *married*. Our family isn't like all those people in the Hollywood columns."

Mark stopped at a red light. "Didn't you tell me your parents were separated?"

"Not legally. Nothing's really decided."

"How long's your father been out here—seven months? Why shouldn't he be involved with some-one?"

"Because he shouldn't have left us in the first place, that's why."

"Us? You're here with him, aren't you?"

"The light's green."

They drove in silence for blocks and blocks. Lucy began to feel embarrassed. Even if Mark didn't understand how she felt about Lynne and her father, there was no reason to be rude.

"I had another big surprise yesterday," Lucy said.

"I guess it isn't a secret anymore since Dad's decided to tell Lorcaster."

Mark's eyebrows were raised as he glanced at Lucy.

"You remember how just before the last take I said my horse had run away with me? That's not what really happened. I was starting back toward the set, and just as I reached the fork, a man raced toward me on an Appaloosa. He forced me onto the other trail and tried to run me off the hill."

"Lucy!"

"I know it sounds wild, but it happened, Mark. Really! I used the trick from the end of our scene and managed to get away. I've never seen Jake, but that's who Dad thought it was from my description."

"Why didn't you say anything? You did the scene as though nothing had happened."

"Dad's had troubles enough on this show already. I didn't want the crew talking all over town."

Mark turned to her with a smile. "I knew you were a gutsy girl that first day we rehearsed the chase scene."

"Not about everything," she said softly.

"So now we know that Jake did the pool."

"Most people think so. But I'm still not sure. I've been finding out all kinds of things about the people on *Malibu*. And I've still more questions to ask."

"Oh? Do you play detective often?"

"Every chance I get." As Mark laughed, Lucy hid a smile. Wouldn't he be surprised to know she'd solved two real mysteries already!

"So, Miss Marple, what intriguing discoveries have you made?"

"Okay, to begin with, when Darci stayed over Tuesday night after Van's party she said she was sure someone had drugged her champagne. She told me she'd have been deathly ill if most of her glass hadn't spilled. You were standing next to her. Did she really spill her drink?"

Mark thought a moment. "Yes. We were both worried about Van's chair. He's very fussy."

"Did anyone get near Darci's glass?"

"Not that I saw. Ross, I think, brought the drink on a tray. It could have been tampered with earlier."

"Well, anyway, if Darci was right—"

"Who knows. She's always making up stories."

"Okay, but if she *was* right, then there's something going on that has nothing to do with Jake. So after Priscilla fell into the pool, I asked myself who else could have a motive for putting insecticide in the water."

"And?"

"Well, according to the script, you and Slade should have been first into the water."

A mischievous grin crossed Mark's face. "And who did you find with a grudge against me?"

"So far, only Timon." Lucy smiled sideways at Mark. "But of course I don't know anything about your private life."

"Yeah, I burn up Timon just by breathing. It probably has to do with the caste system out here. People can't help feeling envious some of the time. But he seems basically a decent guy."

"I found out a few things," Lucy said. "Timon's father was a studio electrician who moonlighted around Malibu. He took his kid along to some of his jobs. Timon's never forgotten the visit to your house. Especially the pony."

"Fantastic. You got all that out of him? He's monosyllabic around me."

"You see what I'm getting at? Timon could have done the pool. He can easily come and go around the club at any time to look after his horses. And he's been making electrical connections since he was a kid, so the paddock gate would have been easy."

"Should I start looking over my shoulder?"

Was he making fun of her? He certainly wasn't taking this seriously.

"Anyway, I haven't found anyone else with a motive for the pool. It seems as though everybody loves Slade."

"Did Darci give you any idea who might have spiked her drink?"

"Not then. But she stayed at the house again Thursday night. Look, you've got to keep my secrets."

"Sure, Lucy, sure."

"Well, Darci has some idea that Ray—and Mavis too—want to do away with her before she's twenty-one. That's when they lose control of her trust fund. If she dies first, the money belongs to Mavis."

"Do you believe that rubbish?"

"I'm not sure. I had a feeling that Darci was making up the story on the spot. But I don't know why she'd want to. There's only one thing I'm sure of—the night of the party, Darci was good and scared of *someone.*"

Mark looked ahead at the road and didn't answer.

Suddenly Lucy felt her ideas were terribly flimsy. And yet, she wasn't ready to let go.

"Look, Lucy," Mark said, "Jake has the strongest motive and he's the only one really implicated. What's more, he's the only one who accounts for the changing targets. Don't forget that no one person has been the intended victim every time. Slade scores one. I score two. And two for Darci or her double. Jake wants to get back at your father. He doesn't care who he hurts —*whom* he hurts—as long as the production's held up and the publicity is damaging. I don't want to discourage you from sleuthing, but—"

"That's okay," Lucy said, trying hard to sound casual. "It's not all that important."

"Well, close the file for today, anyhow. We're here!"

As the car made a turn Lucy noticed acres of low cream-colored buildings with reddish tile roofs—a modern echo of Spanish California—spread out against a backdrop of mountains.

Mark pointed to a huge rectangular structure. "There's a regulation size polo field under there. It's the largest equestrian arena in the world."

Lucy was incredulous as they drove once around the entire spread, past the clubhouse and the many specialized rings for dressage and Grand Prix jumping, for beginners and general riding. Finally they parked near a row of enormous barns.

"You're really going to see something now," Mark said.

Near the center barn, a groom was waiting with one of the most extraordinary horses Lucy had ever seen. He was easily sixteen and a half hands high and as black as the onyx in her mother's necklace. His eyes were bright and he was dancing in place, waiting to get out and go.

"Don't you want to work with him first?" Lucy asked tentatively. Ricochet stood about five and a half feet at the withers. "I've ridden horses this big, but not over fences."

"Good. You'll learn to judge a different stride."

Lucy accepted a leg up and put her mind on what she was doing. Mark would never have let her ride his horse if he hadn't felt they'd be fine together. He led her to a nearby training ring where Doreen Ambling was waiting.

The lesson turned out to be a challenge as well as a treat. For the first fifteen minutes Lucy got the feel of Ricochet while Doreen sized up Lucy's ability. She offered quiet suggestions that helped Lucy put the big horse through a series of figure eights, at a trot and a canter with a smoothness that took her by surprise.

By the time they began to jump a series of low fences, Lucy knew she was making contact with Ricochet's mouth. She was glad to find that her hands were as sensitive as ever. But the long stride was a new sensation, and she had trouble judging the distance between each jump. Catching her uncertainty, Ricochet began to rush the fences, jumping before he received a signal.

Doreen did a lot to straighten them both out before the end of the lesson. They worked over poles laid out on the ground to help Lucy get a better sense of the stride. A good deal of time was spent circling in front of fences without jumping, as well as riding up to the fences and deliberately coming to a halt. Mark watched patiently from the rail through the entire hour, occasionally chatting a bit with people who stopped to say hello.

It was really funny, Lucy thought to herself as she brought Ricochet back to the ring gate. Most people watched you take a jumper over a fence and thought that was the hard part. But the real work was between the fences, getting the horse set up just right.

Mark smiled his approval as Lucy gave him the horse. He introduced Lucy to a skinny blond guy who'd been standing with him for quite a while.

"Lucy Hill, Bob Whitfield."

"You've got real potential," Bob offered. "Not flashy, but real. Your hands are responsive and you've got obvious rapport with the horse."

"Well, thanks," Lucy said politely. She wanted to add, "I'm very rusty," but she bit her tongue. Mr. Kendrick frowned on that kind of apology.

When Bob left, Lucy swung off Ricochet and walked beside Mark toward the barn.

"Bob's an outstanding rider," Mark said quietly. "He's trained at Gladstone."

Lucy's heart flip-flopped. What had he said about her lesson? Gladstone, in New Jersey, was the home of the United States Equestrian Team. Each year leading young riders were chosen to work there for several weeks.

The rest of the afternoon was easy. Nothing bothered her—not her parents and Lynne, not the Malibu mystery, not goofing things up with Mark.

They wandered through the shops in the clubhouse

where everything that was sold, from weather vanes to jewelry, related to horses. Finally they sat down to eat under a striped umbrella on the clubhouse terrace. After a while, Bob Whitfield joined them and Lucy had a great time asking questions about her idols on the USET.

As they sat enjoying the beautiful day, Mark pointed out a wooden square on the scalloped fencing that enclosed the terrace. "You can't read that sign from this side, but it says Only Horses Are Permitted to Jump Over This Fence. *Not* People!"

Lucy laughed. It was a joke, of course. But the way she felt just then, she'd have liked to try it herself!

Chapter Eight

As the weekend went on, Lucy's anger began to boil. At the same time, she was confused. Her father acted as though her blowup over Lynne had never happened. They hadn't talked about it either, even though he'd promised. Somehow they were never alone long enough to get started. Saturday night her grandparents had come over to the Benedict Canyon house. Sunday morning her father fixed brunch for Van and a new *Malibu* writer. In the afternoon they saw a terrific polo game, but the production accountant came along and the two men talked business most of the time.

Sunday dinner was the last straw. As Lucy followed the head waiter into the restaurant, a distinguished older couple waved from a nearby table. During the introductions, Lucy recognized the man's name from talk about Lorcaster. Sure enough, her father couldn't resist the invitation to join them.

By the end of the meal, Lucy knew that she'd been silent to the point of rudeness. Her father was annoyed, but she didn't care.

"You'd better get to bed," he said firmly as they faced one another back in the kitchen at home.

"You've got a big scene tomorrow and the studio car will be here at six thirty."

Lucy started to apologize as he kissed her, but she swallowed the words. There was too much else to say.

"Good night, then," her father said.

"Good night."

As she tried to fall asleep, Lucy's thoughts were as tangled as the branches outside her window, outlined by moonlight against the wall of the canyon. Had her father deliberately avoided being alone with her, or was it really necessary to spend time with all these other people? Why hadn't he told her he was going with Lynne as soon as she'd arrived in California? Did he feel she was too young to understand? Was he afraid she'd carry tales to her mother? Actually, she'd understood some of the problems between her parents for a while now. And her mother had started dating, too. To tell the truth, she liked Lynne.

Lucy sighed and turned over. She should really have been worrying about her big scene with the snake the next day. She'd have to concentrate hard to pull it off.

It was barely light when Lucy and Mr. Hill met in the kitchen the next morning. A glass of orange juice was waiting for her on the table.

"Shall I fix you fried eggs or one of your special pancakes?"

"I'll just get some cold cereal, thanks."

"Then I'm off, honey. I still have to shave."

Lucy drained her glass and fixed herself a bowl of shredded wheat. She thought of another early morning breakfast back in July when her father had told her he might be breaking up with her mother. Afterward they'd driven to Up and Down Farm for a horse show. She'd been terribly upset, but she'd switched the conversation off in her head to concentrate on her riding. Back then, she'd gotten lots of practice putting things out of her head. It was the only way to handle the quarreling and the tension in the house. Funny, she'd forgotten how bad it had been.

As they were driven to Malibu, Lucy leaned back against the seat and looked at her father. He'd gone to sleep. The skin seemed too tight over his high cheekbones and there were black smudges under his eyes. The day of the production meeting he'd been rested and exuberant. What a difference seven days had made.

Without thinking, Lucy put a hand on her father's knee. They'd often driven that way together from the time she was little. Mr. Hill woke with a start. He caught her hand before she could move it away.

"Hi, Dad. This is the first time we've sat together in the back of a limousine!"

Mr. Hill smiled. "I'm glad to have a driver today. I'm feeling my age. But by the end of the week the first thirteen shows will be in the can, and we'll have the union's report on Jake too. I can get a rest. And if Jake's expelled, I can go public about all the trouble he's caused since the explosion."

"I don't get it, Dad. Why not accuse him now? The police could question him, at least."

"Because I haven't any proof. Whatever I say will seem like unfair pressure on the union to back me up on the charges I've made."

He turned to Lucy. "The trouble is that by the time

I'm ready to relax, you'll be flying back to New York. I don't think I've been fair to you, honey. I've been preoccupied and worried from the time you got here."

She started to protest but he motioned for silence. "I know you want to talk about Lynne and me. It's funny. Usually I'm the one who tries to get you to talk things out and you're the one who clams up—or eats pickles, like that time in Lindy's when I told you I was coming out here. You ate the whole bowl, Mite. I don't think I'll ever get that awful lunch scene out of my mind. I hated to see you so upset.

"Well, this time, I'm the one who can't seem to talk. For weeks now I've had to put my personal life on hold and concentrate on work."

"I know what you mean! I did something like that last summer, when you and Mom were breaking up and I was trying to qualify as an Open rider."

"Well, then, please Mite. Let's leave it alone. I still have a lot of problems to solve and you have your big scene with the snake today. Believe me, there's really nothing you need to know right now—except that you come first with me, no matter what."

Lucy leaned back against the seat, surprised at her relief. What had Mark said? "You're here with him, aren't you?" That was the important part. Whatever was going on between her father and mother or her father and Lynne wasn't really her problem. It wasn't for her to work out.

The car was making the turn onto the Pacific Coast Highway. Lucy took her hand from her father's knee and pointed up to the hill. "Have you ever been to the Getty Museum?"

"No."

"Let's go there together sometime." She reached over and kissed her father's cheek. "I love you a lot."

He didn't answer. She could see from his face that he couldn't.

"Say, Dad. Since you're the producer, could you get the caterer to give us some pickles for lunch? I promise I'll only eat one."

It wasn't exactly a brilliant line, but she'd tried. Her father laughed and shifted in his seat as though able to relax for the first time.

Lucy put her mind on the snake scene. It was like all those other early mornings on the way to horse shows when, after they'd chatted a bit, she'd review the points she was supposed to remember for the day. Let's see, Timon had said, "Free your feet from the stirrups before you reach your mark, grab a small piece of the mane, and signal Durkin to rear." It was time to concentrate on her own business.

"Meet your co-star," Timon said as Lucy stared into the snake's open jaws.

A flour sack lay on the ground as the animal handler held up the long, gray-brown rattler. The white markings along its body looked like circles of teeth.

"You see, no fangs," he said. "I'm going to put him in a cage and find a shady place to leave him."

"Lucy, this is Jerry Krater," Timon said. The three of them looked around the flat ridge where the snake scene was to be filmed after lunch. Timon and Lucy had been practicing there for the past hour. Today the padding would be thinner and under her clothes, so she'd had to get used to the difference. When Jerry's van had driven into the parking lot, they'd tied up the horses and come over to talk.

"Is that Edgar?" Timon asked Jerry.

"No, a new guy—J.R. I couldn't bring Edgar because they didn't want the fangs."

"You know Jerry already?" Lucy said to Timon, as she watched the handler close the cage door on J.R.

"Yeah, we've worked together before. Besides, I had to teach Durkin not to spook at snakes. I bought two different rattlers from Jerry."

Lucy stared at the cage.

"So this snake can't bite, huh?"

"Sure he can bite," Jerry said.

"But didn't you—"

"I said he was defanged." Jerry looked at Timon and shrugged. "I'd better give her the lecture. First of all, there's some idea that people die from snake bites all the time. The truth is, only about three percent of the people who are bitten by poisonous snakes die. The chances are even better if they're near medical attention.

"Now about the fangs. They're really special teeth that fold up against the roof of the mouth. When the snake bites, they move forward and release the venom. But even if the fangs are removed, a snake's got its other teeth. It can strike and it can bite. No poison will be released but the bite hurts plenty."

"Take it easy," Timon said. "She's the girl who's doing the scene today."

Jerry looked at Lucy with new interest. "Oh, well, you won't have any trouble. Rattlers don't usually bother anyone unless they're bothered first. Someone moves a log where they're hiding, someone steps on them in the grass. Otherwise they mostly rest, coiled up like a garden hose. I'm just hoping J.R. will perform at all. The director told me he wants a couple of close shots of him in a striking coil, but snakes can be sluggish on a hot day."

"It's hot, all right," Lucy said, thinking that the padding only made it worse.

Jerry looked superior. "You think it's hot? Be glad you're not a snake. People have thermostats. Snakes just get hot and cold depending where they are. That's why I'm looking for some shade."

He pointed to a group of rocks about fifty yards away that formed a small shelter. "There's a spot. Good-bye for now. My call is for one o'clock and I've got to eat lunch."

"Us too," Timon said. "See ya, Jerry."

"How close do I get to the snake?" Lucy asked Timon as they started back to the stable trail.

"Not very. Not if you do a good job and bring the horse to your mark. After the fall, remember, you'll hold your position till the end of the take. The snake will be lying coiled up in the background. Just forget about it."

"I'd like to hear him rattle."

"Look, Lucy, forget the snake. We've got to eat. I've got to clean up Durkin too. Let's move."

Lucy followed Timon at a fast trot and forced herself to think about lunch.

After lunch, Lucy could hardly sit still as Guy put on her makeup. To her surprise, she found the whole process fascinating. He made her skin look perfectly smooth and her eyes much bigger. The makeup made her seem older. Too bad Allison couldn't see her now. Maybe someday she'd get one of those demonstrators in the stores to teach her what to use herself.

"Sit still, Lucy," Guy said.

"Sorry. I'm too excited."

"You've been at this a few days already."

"I know, but today's the day that counts."

He put a final touch to her mouth. "Too bad they won't see your face. Don't you look marvelous?"

"Thanks. You do a great job, Guy."

After "Makeup" was through with her, Rick fussed with her hair and "Wardrobe" helped her to put all the pads in place—on her hipbones and rear, even on her knees and elbows.

As she finally hurried toward the door, Wardrobe handed her a crop. "Remember, forget about your clothes and play the scene. We've got a second set of everything if you need them."

A navy blue Cadillac was parked beside the trailer and the Mexican driver rushed to open the door. Darci was already in the back seat, dressed in a green short-sleeved shirt, blue jeans, chaps, and a hunt cap, exactly like Lucy. It was strange. Lucy felt she was staring at a picture of herself taken four years in the future.

"You look good in makeup," Darci said without a hello. "You're really very pretty."

"Do I? I'm not really used to this stuff on my face."

"Get used to it, then. Couldn't you see yourself in the dressing table mirror?" Darci frowned. "You're a good kid, Lucy, but you're a little weird."

So are you, friend, Lucy thought. She watched Darci try to light a cigarette with one match after another.

"What's the matter, Darci? You're shaking."

"I'm terrified! But how could you understand? You *like* the silly beasts."

"What are you afraid of? You don't have to ride."

"Thanks a lot. After you fall off and walk away, I do the close shots on the ground. *I'm* the one the horse will step on."

"Honestly, Darci, horses never step on people if they can help it. And Durkin's been trained to—"

"Then he'll bite me. They've got those awful teeth." Darci took a deep breath and stared out of the car window.

Lucy kept quiet. Nothing she'd say was going to make a difference.

"Lucy, it's not just the horse." The ash from Darci's cigarette dropped onto the car floor.

"Well, what then? Jake can't get near us today. The action's all in one place and we'll be surrounded by detectives."

"Lucy." Darci put a hand on Lucy's arm. "There's one thing I hate more than horses and that's snakes."

"So that's it. But it's not a real rattler, Darci."

"Of course it is."

"I mean, it's defanged. It can't hurt you."

"Okay, so I won't die of snake poisoning. I'll die of a heart attack just looking at the thing."

"I was at the location this morning, Darci, when the snake arrived. It was beautiful in an ugly sort of way."

"Don't talk about it or I'll be dead before we get there."

The Mexican driver burst out laughing.

"Don't you dare laugh at me!" Darci snapped.

"Sorry, señorita. Sorry."

"You'd better be."

Lucy was relieved to get to the set. Two detectives met them at the car and asked for identification.

Darci said irritably, "You saw me this morning at the Malibu pier. I'm Darci Rutland. And she's Lucy Hill, the producer's daughter."

The detectives motioned them on and Lucy checked the scene. Some of the crew called out greetings or waved hello. Timon was holding Durkin and listening to Van's instructions.

"The snake will be about there. When the horse rears, Lucy should land in a heap about four feet away. I've worked the scene out carefully with the handler. We won't start the action until the snake's in a 'resting coil.' Then he'll stay that way, unless he's frightened."

"Good afternoon, ladies," Van interrupted his own monologue. "Timon's running through the scene to show Ross the action. We're trying to spare you, Lucy, but pay attention."

Darci flopped into a folding chair with her name stenciled across the back. Lucy listened hard.

"All right, Durkin ends up standing over Lucy who holds her position on the ground until I say cut. Later we'll do separate close-ups of lunging snake and terrified Darci. Questions?"

Darci looked off toward the parked cars as if plotting an escape. "Oh, Lord, that's all I need!" she suddenly groaned. Ray and Mavis were approaching the set.

Van stepped behind the camera, "Timon, let me watch it one time all the way."

Lucy was no longer surprised when "one time" turned into four. She registered Timon's every move, suddenly filled with regret that this would be her last scene. She was getting to like this crazy business. And it was exciting to be involved with so many skilled people at work, people who enjoyed what they were doing and delivered every time.

I'll make this scene spectacular, Lucy vowed. Throwing yourself into a scene wasn't all that different from going into the show ring, she thought. You pulled your energy and your cool together much the same way. Maybe anything you took seriously taught you about other things too. Like now. *Concentrate,* Mr. Kendrick's favorite word, was the best advice here. In fact, Timon used it a lot too.

There were three things to get right. Hit her mark, leave the horse at the exact moment, and make the fall look natural. She'd gone over it all again and again in her mind. Now was the time just to *do* it.

"Is Lucy ready?" Van called. "Let's watch her once."

"All set, Van," Timon called when she'd settled into the saddle.

The rehearsal went perfectly, and Lucy couldn't

wait for the take. Durkin seemed to catch her excitement, playing with the bit and prancing in place as she dusted herself off and looked for Timon.

"Exactly like that. Again," Timon said, taking Durkin's reins. Lucy was suddenly surrounded. Wardrobe freshened up her clothes with a portable hand vacuum. Makeup dusted her face. The hairdresser adjusted her ponytail and straightened her hunt cap.

"Stoke yourselves up," Van said, as the camera operator peered through the eyepiece. "Let's go for it."

Lucy climbed into the saddle and listened to the familiar routine. "Places everybody."

"Roll sound."

"Speed."

"Camera"

"Speed"

"Mark it."

The assistant director held a small slate in front of the camera with the production and scene numbers chalked on it. He banged the clapsticks at the top together loudly so that, later, the sound and the picture could be lined up exactly.

Lucy patted Durkin's neck and tightened her fingers on the reins.

"All right, Lucy. *Action.*"

Timon waved her forward and she cantered to her mark. She gave Durkin his cue and he reared high, his front legs pawing the air. Staying on till the last possible second, she looked down at the snake from between Durkin's ears. It was all coiled up, resting in the sun.

The crop flipped out of Lucy's hand, but the fall

was perfect. She huddled on the ground trying to appear unconscious until Van yelled, *"Cut."* When she looked up, the snake was slithering toward her.

He's defanged, Lucy reminded herself. It's only J.R., probably frightened by the crop. She was mesmerized as the long forked tongue whipped up and down and the whir of the rattle magnified in her ears. Suddenly, the snake coiled again and raised its head straight in the air. In an instant it lunged across several feet to land openmouthed against Lucy's leg.

It withdrew as fast as it had struck.

Lucy stared at her chap.

"Help!" she yelled. "Somebody come *quick!*"

Chapter Nine

Timon came running. "The scene looked great, Lucy. But your crop scared J.R. Did he bite you? It looked as though he only got your chap."

Lucy took a deep breath and managed to sputter, "It's the wrong snake. Watch out, Timon!"

"What happened, Lucy?" Her father pushed past Timon to bend over her.

"Look, Dad." A trickle of venom was drying on the leather below her knee.

"What the hell's going on here. Wasn't that snake fixed up?" Mr. Hill shouted.

The animal handler ran toward them. "He was fixed, all right. The riding crop scared him so he lunged, but there's no—"

Timon grabbed Jerry's shoulder. "What kind of a jerk are you anyway? Look, there's venom! There, on her leg!"

The handler's cheek began to twitch. "Impossible. There can't be venom without fangs. That snake has no fangs." But Jerry bent over Lucy's leg as he protested. He stood up slowly, staring at the snake lying quietly about twelve feet away. Then he turned and bolted for his van with two detectives right behind him.

Mr. Hill helped Lucy up and took her in his arms. Neither one of them spoke. As they broke apart, Lucy looked for Durkin. He was still standing in place just as he'd been trained to do.

As Timon led the horse away Jerry hurried back, flanked by the detectives. He carried a long pole with a leather loop on the end. Carefully drawing the loop over the snake's head, he scooped it into the cage.

"You're some lucky guy," Mr. Hill said, the color still drained from his face. "If my daughter'd been hurt, I'd have wrapped that snake around your throat."

Lucy reached toward her father. "It's okay, Dad. Really. I'm okay."

Jerry was trembling as he approached Mr. Hill. "This is terrible. I know I brought a defanged snake this morning. Ask your daughter. She met J.R. before lunch."

Lucy nodded quickly. "That's true, Dad. He showed me."

"So where did the snake go for lunch? And where were you at the time?"

"I left him in his cage under the rocks." He pointed off in the direction of the parking lot. "The van's too hot out in the sun."

Mr. Hill turned to the security guards. "Who was up here during lunch break?"

They began to look uncomfortable.

"No one?"

"Mr. Hill," one of them said. "We didn't know we

107

had a snake to look after up here. The morning shoot was at the fishing pier."

Her father sighed. "You've got a point."

Van put a hand on Mr. Hill's shoulder. "Allan, we can go with Lucy's scene. Now all we need are close-ups of the snake and close-ups of Darci. The snake won't be near her at any time. Can't we keep on going? Ask Jerry what he thinks."

"Can we work with this snake?" Mr. Hill asked.

"Sure. I can handle him," Jerry said.

"Now where's Darci?" Van said. *"Darci!"*

A production assistant came running. "She fainted, Van. Her mother's putting cold towels on her forehead up at the prop truck."

Mr. Hill clutched his head.

"I'll get her, Mr. Hill. Right away."

A detective called over to Jerry, who was examining the snake. "How far away are those rocks where you parked the cage?"

"Come on. I'll show you."

"No, he can't leave!" Van insisted. "We're going to finish the sequence."

"I can take you there," Lucy volunteered.

"No you can't," Van said loudly. "We may need your help to match these scenes." He called the script supervisor over. "Did you get Lucy's exact position on the ground?"

Feeling a bit shaky, Lucy sat down in Darci's chair. She stood up again quickly as Darci approached.

"You can stay there," Darci said. "You know, until I got up real close, I thought I saw myself sitting there." She cocked her head at Lucy. "Am I glad it was you the snake went for and not me!"

They were look-alikes, all right. And so they were both in danger. But there was more to it than that. Had Jake found out that Darci had a double? Would he have cared which one of them was bitten? Probably not. Jake had two ways to hurt her father—through his production and through his daughter.

"Mark? Hi, it's Lucy." She relaxed her grip on the receiver. "Am I glad you're still in Malibu. I was afraid you'd left for Beverly Hills."

"I'll be here another few hours. How did it go today?"

"That's why I'm calling. It was crazy, Mark. The handler brought this defanged snake named J.R. to the location in the morning, but someone switched it for a different snake at lunchtime, and when I did my scene—"

"Hey, Lucy. Take a deep breath and tell me slowly."

"We're friends, right?"

"Of course we're friends."

"Well, I need to ask you a favor."

There was silence at the other end of the line.

"I guess I shouldn't have asked," Lucy said quickly. "Forget it. I'll—"

"Easy, Lucy. I was just drinking my coffee. Keep going."

"I told you that someone switched snakes during the lunch break. Well, the poisonous snake *attacked* me. If I hadn't been wearing chaps I'd have been bitten. You could see the venom."

"No wonder you're worked up. What do you want me to do?"

"Wait a minute." Lucy checked the hallway from the guest room door and came back to the phone.

"Dad's in a hurry to get out of here and back to Benedict Canyon. He said the detectives saw prints of unusual horseshoes around the rocks where the snake was left."

"What was unusual about them?"

"I don't know. But that's what the detectives said, 'unusual.' I want to check out those prints for myself."

"*Now* I get it." Mark laughed. "This call is from Miss Marple!"

"I hoped you could drive me up there. And I need an excuse to get out of the house."

"Can't you just tell your father the truth?"

"He'll think I'm butting in. He's been in knots all week and this afternoon just made it worse."

"I have an idea. She isn't here, but I'll call you back and you can say I asked you down to meet Rita. I don't think your father will say no to that."

"He wants to leave in an hour."

"See if you can stretch it. In any case, I know my way up and down those roads. We'll make it."

It was beautiful up in the hills as the early evening light softened the edges of the mountains and canyons. "Why are we going to the ravine?" Mark asked, as the Porsche breezed up the slope. "Didn't we start out for the rocks where the snake was left at lunchtime?"

"First of all, it's on the way. I thought we'd check at the side of the ravine where Jake tried to run me off the trail. Some of those hoofprints should still be there. The point is, I want to match up the two sets of prints."

"So if the same 'unusual' horseshoe print shows up in both places, you'll conclude that Jake switched the snakes?"

"Of course."

Mark parked the car near the chase location and smiled at Lucy. "Here goes." That smile was really getting to her. How could you feel weak at the knees when you were sitting down?

They locked up the car. The ocean stretched in front of them, still and intriguing, as the clear blues and greens of the afternoon deepened to a magical gray. Mark stood beside her quietly, also caught up in watching the sea. It was hard for Lucy to keep her mind on why she was there.

As they walked the left-hand fork of the trail, they looked for unusual prints, but if any had been there before, they were now covered with dry dust and the tracks of weekend riders.

Lucy went on ahead around the hill, to the spot where Jake had pressed her off the path. Suddenly, her legs began to wobble. The ravine, filled with shadows, was strangely ominous. She stopped in her tracks and waited for Mark.

"You okay?" he asked.

"I guess so."

"Keep your eyes on the ground." His head was bent as he moved to the side of the trail.

"Say, Luce, look here!"

Luce. Her brother's pet name for her. She forced herself to follow Mark's finger.

"You can see exactly what happened. Durkin's prints are here, and the Appaloosa's too. What's more, Jake's horse had bar shoes on his front feet."

Lucy kneeled down to look more closely. There was the mark of an extra rectangular piece across the opening of the shoe. She'd seen them once at Mr. Kendrick's on a horse with an injured tendon.

They walked along together, tracing the Appaloosa's long stride. Then Lucy straightened up and took a deep breath.

"Okay! We're halfway."

Mark smiled. "Now it gets harder. I don't know where you worked with the snake."

"Mark," she moaned. "That never occurred to me! But I'm sure we went farther up this road. Let's just drive along and see."

"I hope you're right. We told your Dad we'd be back in an hour. If he phones my house he'll know that we lied."

They'd driven just a few minutes when Lucy grabbed Mark's knee. "Stop. The cars were parked over there."

"We're in luck," Mark said, as Lucy led the way to the triangle of rocks. "The detectives are gone and there's no one around."

Lucy looked up the road. "The prints start over there. Why didn't the rider use the trail?"

"People ride on the road sometimes."

They bent to examine the hoofprints nearby. "Well, what do you think?" Mark said.

"I'm not sure."

"*I* am. They're the same prints, all right. Now we know it was Jake."

Lucy didn't answer.

Mark looked at her, puzzled. "It's a bar shoe and so was the one at the ravine. There's no question about that."

"I know. But look, Mark. Look at how these prints lie in the dirt. Jake's horse was big and heavy. These prints should be deeper. And does the stride look right to you?"

"It's hard to tell. Up at the ravine, the horse was galloping. Here it was walking."

Carefully Mark and Lucy studied the pattern of prints going from the rocks to the road. The further they went, the more certain Lucy became that something was wrong.

"These may be the same kind of horseshoes, Mark, but I'll bet you anything they weren't on the same horse."

"I'm beginning to think you're right."

Mark ran ahead, his eyes on the ground. At the edge of the road, he called to Lucy.

"Come check the walking pattern here. It doesn't look right."

It certainly didn't. "Mark, there's half a stride missing in at least two places!"

"Hey, Luce—Miss Marple—whoever you are. We're on to something!"

"You bet we are! I don't know how these prints got

here," Lucy said, "but they weren't made by a horse at all!"

"It's crazy. How do you explain it?"

"Someone looked at the prints up on the left-hand trail—"

"And saw their chance to use Jake for cover! Wow. You've said all along that we shouldn't pin everything on Jake."

Lucy smiled to herself. "It was only a crazy hunch."

"Well, I'm impressed. We'll get together when everyone's back in L.A. and sort things out."

She felt she'd won a blue ribbon in a very special class.

Chapter Ten

"We'll leave for the studio at seven o'clock," Mr. Hill said Tuesday morning over breakfast. "Are you sleepy?"

"No, Dad. I'm fine."

He studied her closely. "You look as though you spent the night dreaming about snakes."

Lucy didn't answer. Actually, the trouble had been getting to sleep at all. She'd felt peculiar about lying to her father when she'd gone off with Mark. And he would have to know she'd lied. How else could she tell him about the hoofprints, and that a second culprit was hiding behind Jake. She'd been stewing, too, about who that could be. When would the next move come? Who would be the target?

The phone rang. It was already the third business call that morning.

"Why, hello, Mavis," her father said. "Yes, I'm on my way to the studio now."

Lucy listened carefully, over the crunching of the toast in her mouth.

"Now, Mavis, of course I understand that the whole episode was a shock. But we're a day behind schedule already. I think you should persuade Darci to get over to the studio right away. There's nothing to worry about. We'll have security on the set and Jake can't even get through the gate."

Her father listened, then sighed loudly. "All right, you get Darci to the studio in the next half hour and I'll see that she has her own protection. Yes, I understand. Good-bye, Mavis."

"That girl has to go," Mr. Hill said as he hung up the phone. "I don't know why Van's so convinced that she adds to the show. After this new batch of scripts I think I'll have Calloway Martin ship her back East. Or we'll arrange a fatal accident."

"Hey, Dad. I wouldn't joke that way. You almost got your wish in real life."

"Not with Darci, I didn't. With her double, who happens to be my daughter. I'd like to tear Jake apart with my bare hands."

"Wow, you're fierce today!"

Should she tell him about the phony hoofprints now? Lucy wondered. If she and Mark were right about the prints being fake, someone besides Jake was a real source of danger. Her father should know. And yet she hated to add to his worries without proof he could use. By now the faulty prints near the road were probably tracked over or blown away.

The phone rang again and made the decision for her. As her father began to talk, Lucy left the table.

When they walked through the door of Soundstage D, Lucy still hadn't mentioned the hoofprints. Mr. Hill waved toward the cavernous studio. "You have just entered the world of Calloway Martin, her family, friends and foes.

"Shall we pay a visit to the Beverly Hills mansion, or the million dollar beach house in Malibu? Or would you rather see the unpretentious digs where grandson Paul conjures up his vicious schemes, or . . ."

As her father rattled on, Lucy stared at the vast area filled with sections of rooms. "Now, this is the library-office from which Calloway Martin reigns. Of course we add some props for each show, but the basic set stays in place." Mr. Hill laughed. "At least it does until we're kicked off the air."

Lucy picked out the decanter and brandy glasses on a drum table, Trivial Pursuit on a bookshelf. She was amused to step off the oriental rug in the "library" onto the bare concrete floor of the soundstage.

In the "dining room," where the morning's work was going to take place, the prop people were setting the table.

"This will be fun, Dad. Is the meal breakfast, lunch or dinner?"

"Darci, that is, Jessica, is lunching with Calloway, her grandmother. Only I hope lunch will be served at" —he looked at his watch—"at nine A.M."

"Good morning, Lucy, Allan, everybody." Lynne appeared from behind the office flats.

Above the chorus of replies, Mr. Hill asked, "Is Darci out of makeup yet?"

"Oh yes. Sulking in her dressing room."

"You got the lab report on yesterday's footage?"

"No problems. You can see everything at five."

"Good. You'll finally see yourself in action, Lucy."

"That's great."

"And by the way," Lynne said to Lucy, "I just

117

bumped into Priscilla. I told you she'd get work right away. She's on Soundstage A, if you want to say hello."

"Lynne," Mr. Hill said, "I had to promise Darci her own bodyguard. That's your next joyful chore. If you'll just fix Lucy up with a chair first."

"Don't worry about me, Dad."

Her father didn't seem to hear as Van walked up and broke into rapid-fire speech.

Lynne found a folding chair for Lucy and set it up. Lucy felt uncomfortable because they hadn't seen each other since the blowup in Malibu the week before.

"Lynne, I'm really sorry about the other night. I was—"

"I understand you, Lucy. Forget about it." Lynne smiled and reached out for her arm.

For a moment they looked at each other steadily. Then Lynne left for her office. Lucy settled into her chair and surveyed the scene. She was uneasy about her feelings toward the *Malibu* crowd, whom she'd been friendly with all week. It seemed disloyal to view them all with suspicion, and yet she had no choice.

Slade and Darci began their lunch at ten thirty—an hour and a half later than Mr. Hill had hoped. Underneath her father's icy control, Lucy could see that he was seething. To dress the set, to get the lights just right and to block the shots seemed to take forever. Van was unhappy with Darci's performance and asked for more rehearsal, but finally Mr. Hill insisted they go for a take.

"Darci," Van pleaded. "Slade has nothing to work

off. She can't build a scene all by herself. You're supposed to be quarreling."

After each attempt Van turned away from the set and walked in a little circle.

At the end of the fifth take, he exploded. "Darci, will you give us a *little* energy. Just enough to show us you're alive."

Darci bristled. "Lay off Van. If you showed some respect for my ability as an actress, you'd get a better performance."

Lucy wondered how Darci expected to get a part in Van's feature if she was going to be so difficult.

"Darci, love, we all have days like this," Slade said finally. "Shall we break for ten minutes? Why not come to my dressing room and we'll work together quietly."

"Don't patronize me," Darci lashed out at Slade. "You're always acting like the den mother around here. Well, I've got one mother too many already."

As Slade turned away, Mr. Hill walked onto the set and spoke to Darci quietly. She clenched her jaw and stamped off to her dressing room.

Lucy stared after her. Of course Darci must be especially nervous right now. It wasn't reassuring to have someone drop a poisonous snake into your scene. If she'd been afraid the night of the party she must be even more scared now.

Still, it was hard to believe that Darci had ever been the adorable little girl she remembered in *The Little Soldier*. Lucy would certainly like to see her in that film again. Priscilla had said something about having a tape. Maybe she would go over and say hello.

Lucy suddenly stopped short. The night after the pool accident her father had said none of Darci's early pictures had ever been released on video cassette. That was interesting. Had she misunderstood Priscilla? Or could her father have been mistaken? Lucy's mind began to play with the new questions. If Priscilla was free for lunch, she'd try for the answers.

"Thanks for your get well card," Priscilla said to Lucy as they sat together in the studio commissary.

"I'm glad you feel better. When did you finally get out of the hospital?"

"Friday morning. I was lucky. The call for this job came in Friday too. It's a television movie with all sorts of big stars. What more can I ask?"

"Since your accident, some more things have happened around the *Malibu* set that weren't in the script."

"Such as?"

"Such as Van almost getting electrocuted, me almost getting shoved into a ravine, and, last but not least, me almost getting bitten by a poisonous rattler."

"That's what you get for being Darci's double."

"Yeah. That got through to me after a while."

"It's all being blamed on Jake, I guess."

"That's the general idea."

Priscilla was oddly quiet.

"What's the matter?" Lucy asked.

"I'm thinking about something."

"Are you going to tell me?"

"I'm not sure. Why did you want to see me?"

"I wanted to take you up on your offer. The first

120

day we met at my Dad's house, you said you could show me one of Darci's films."

"I did, yeah. So what?"

"You mean you have your own video cassette of *The Little Soldier?*"

"No. I can get it, that's all."

"How come?"

"It's no big deal, Lucy. My boyfriend, Pokey, has a copy. He told me when he heard I was working with Darci on *Malibu.* I can ask him to let you have it for a while."

"That would be great. Do you know where he got it?"

"I didn't bother to ask. He works at a small tape house called TapeDupe. You know, one of those places that copies and edits videotapes. He's a sound engineer, with incredible ears for frequencies and decibels. But between his ears he's pretty spacey. He's worked at better places but he always goofs up somehow."

"Maybe they copied the picture where he works."

"Could be. Knowing him, he probably just ran off an extra tape for himself."

"Do you think I could meet Pokey?"

"What on earth for?"

Lucy grabbed the first idea that came into her head. "Well, that tape would make a great present for Van when the shoot's over. I guess you call it a 'wrap present.' "

"Wait a *min*ute. I'm not going to get Pokey into trouble. No way. He may be a space cadet at times, but he *is* my boyfriend."

"Why should this get Pokey into trouble? He can

just get another tape the way he got the first one. Of course, we'll pay him for it."

Priscilla was shredding the paper napkin on her tray. "Look, forget about this whole thing. Don't drag Pokey or me into this tape business in any way. If that was the reason you wanted to have lunch, I'm sorry I said yes."

"Hey, Priscilla, please don't be angry. I thought it would be fun to talk and, yeah, I wanted to see the tape too."

Priscilla stood up. "I've got to go."

Lucy hated to leave it like that.

"Well, can't we at least walk back together? I guess I could get from the commissary to Stage D but I'd have to ask a lot of directions."

Priscilla sighed. "Yeah—well—come on."

As Lucy stood up, Priscilla looked at her curiously. "What sign were you born under anyway?"

"Taurus. Why?"

"I'm into astrology. I make a lot of decisions by the stars."

What was Priscilla debating? Before they left the table, Lucy noticed her tray. The shreds of paper had been rolled into tight little balls. Evidently Priscilla's horoscope wasn't so favorable today.

Chapter Eleven

"Lynne, I really want to thank you for taking the time this afternoon," Lucy said as they drove to TapeDupe. "You're busy every second and—"

"No problem. We may be on to something important."

Lucy was still surprised at how things had worked out. The night before, she'd been doing the dishes with Lynne. Somehow she'd told her about Priscilla and the video cassette of *The Little Soldier.* That had led to the *Malibu* mystery and in the end Lynne had suggested driving to TapeDupe today.

"It's not just the time I appreciate," Lucy said. "It's that you took me seriously. I don't have much to go on."

"You're making sense. There's no way to be sure that Darci was drugged, but I can certainly accept your judgment about the hoofprints. We don't have any idea if today's trip will connect up with all that, but let's take one step at a time."

Lucy peered out of the car window at the clothing stores along the avenue.

"There are some great shops along here with very

trendy clothes," Lynne said. "We could come back Saturday and shop together, if you like."

"All my allowance goes into boots and show clothes, but it would be fun to look."

"I'm sure your Dad will stake you to a rag or two."

"Then it's a date. Thanks."

Actually, Lucy had been thinking more about clothes lately. Studying her "twin" in different outfits had made her want to experiment.

Gradually the clothing stores and expensive antique shops changed to nondescript storefronts. Lucy kept an eye out for number 6006.

"When are you going to tell Dad about the hoof-prints and the rest?"

"Let it ride, Lucy. You told *me* these things to spare your father. Now the responsibility's mine. When we get around to telling him, Allan will understand."

"I just saw five thousand eighty. We're almost there. How are you going to get Pokey to talk to us?"

"I've been wondering about that. I think I'll play it your way—the wrap present for the director."

"Won't Pokey be furious at Priscilla?"

"If there's something illegal going on and Pokey's part of it, let him get angry. She'd be better off without him."

"I suppose."

Lucy put a hand on the dashboard suddenly. "We must have passed it. I just saw six thousand twelve. I don't understand. I was sure I was watching carefully."

"Don't worry. We'll park the car and walk back."

Number 6006 was a dreary building as run-down as

its neighbors. Small gold numbers were peeling above the mail slot on the rippled-glass door.

"The door's locked," Lynne said, pushing against it.

"Here's a buzzer."

"Go ahead."

Moments later a voice called through the intercom, "TapeDupe. Good afternoon."

"Hello. It's Lynne Stokes from Lorcaster."

"We're one flight up."

The door was released. They stepped into a dingy hallway with an elevator to one side. Without a word they both headed for the stairs in front of them.

"I don't believe it!" Lucy exclaimed, as they pushed open the heavy door at the top of the landing. The hallway was expensively decorated in orange and silver. A sophisticated TapeDupe logo was painted in black and orange on double office doors.

"Maybe they're completely legit," Lynne said.

"Or they're putting on a good show."

Lynne pushed another button and they were buzzed into the reception room. It was small but attractive, with posters of Michael Jackson, David Bowie, Sting, and other rock stars around the walls. A tall thin man in his thirties stood up behind a large desk. He was blond and handsome except for prominent buck teeth.

"What can I do for you? We don't usually get the big guns of the industry out here, Ms. Stokes."

"I suppose, but this is personal. My boyfriend used to make commercials in New York and now he's trying to get started in California. His sample reel's on film and that's a mistake. I'm sure you transfer film to video tape."

"Of course. We're a full service tape house."

Lucy tried not to look at Lynne. What had started her off on this? How would it lead to Pokey? They seemed to be on the wrong track altogether.

"I want to save money," Lynne went on, "but at Lorcaster I'm used to the best. Priscilla Jones, the script supervisor on one of our shows, recommended one of your sound engineers, a guy named Pokey. This reel is heavy on sound effects and—"

"We can match what you get from any outfit in town," Buckteeth said.

"I'm delighted. Could I talk to Pokey?"

"I can answer your questions."

"Yes, but I want him to give this his special attention."

"Look, Ms. Stokes, I run a business here. Mr. Brockaw is busy."

Well, Lucy thought, we have Pokey's last name. Otherwise we're no place.

"Thank you very much, then." Lynne motioned Lucy toward the door.

Buckteeth hesitated. "Just a minute. I'll see what Pokey's doing."

When he'd left the room, Lucy whispered, "Good for you! Now what?"

Lynne turned up her palms.

Lucy walked over to a stack of film and TV magazines piled up on a small table. The *Variety* was three weeks old. The *Millimeter* four months.

The door to the back section opened and a dark-haired young man about four years younger than Priscilla hesitated at the other side of the room. The expression on his perfectly round face was completely bland. His large round eyes checked out the space like an animal's.

"Hello, there. We're friends of Priscilla's," Lynne said warmly.

"But she doesn't know we're here." Lucy added, then wished she could swallow her tongue.

"Yeah, Jimmy told me who you were."

Lucy anxiously watched the door to the back. They were lucky that Jimmy hadn't come back so far.

"I can't talk now," Pokey said. "I'm real busy."

"But this is business," Lynne said. "I've a very tricky reel to transfer to tape and the sound is what makes it special. I hoped you could show us your equipment."

"The equipment's all tied up today. What did you say your name was?"

"Lynne Stokes, and this is Lucy Hill. Her father's the producer of *Malibu.*"

"Tell me about the reel you want me to work on. Maybe I should take it out back and look at the problems."

"We miss Priscilla on *Malibu.* She's good at her job, and fun to have around."

"Yeah, well forget that one. She got a rotten break on that show."

"Oh? I'm sorry to hear you say that. She was completely covered for—"

"I'm glad she's out of there."

Come on, Lynne, get to the point, Lucy found herself urging silently. Buckteeth Jimmy will be back any minute.

"Pokey, we want to be fair," Lynne insisted. "Tell me why you say that."

"Prune isn't talking so I'm not talking. Just let me see the reel."

"Lynne, I think you left it in the car," Lucy said quickly.

"No, Lucy, I'm sure it's in my pocketbook. It's only a small reel." Lynne patted the large tote bag she carried. "Anyway, one more thing before we get to that. Our director, Van Fortune, made a lot of early movies with Darci Rutland. The wrap party for the first thirteen shows is on Friday and I'd like to give him a present of *The Little Soldier.* I thought you could tell me where to get a copy."

"Me! Why me?"

"Somehow I got the idea that you had a copy."

"Where'd you get an idea like that?"

Pokey's pale skin flushed, and one eyelid began to twitch.

"It's not important who told me. It's such a simple matter."

"Look, lady. You're wrong all the way. Now get lost."

He stepped up close and began hustling them toward the door.

"There's no reason to be rude," Lynne said calmly.

The door slammed behind them.

For a moment they stood in the hall just looking at each other.

"Something's wrong here without question," Lynne said. "Pokey acts like a guy who's been told to clam up." They walked back to the steps. "Let me think out what to do next. Also what and when to tell your father. We'll talk about it again later."

Lucy wasn't going to leave it at that. Today was Wednesday and her flight home was on Sunday. Mark had promised to see her the next day. She crossed her fingers and made a pledge. Somehow, she'd solve the mystery before Sunday.

Chapter Twelve

"La Brea is Spanish for tar," Mark said to Lucy. Thursday morning, they stood together at the famous La Brea excavation site, where a treasure of prehistoric animal bones had been found. In the middle of the "lake pit," the life-size model of a saber-toothed mastodon seemed strangely out of place against the background of modern high-rise buildings surrounding Hancock Park.

"I expected real gooey tar, Mark. This is more like oily water."

"Well, the gooey stuff—asphalt really—used to bubble up years ago and harden. This spot here was an old asphalt mine that filled up again with oil and water."

Mark's voice was enthusiastic. "Around nineteen hundred, geologists started to find bones in the asphalt pits. Animals had come to pools like this, thousands of years ago, and been trapped in the gooey stuff underneath."

I hope we don't get stuck in tar ourselves, Lucy thought. We've a lot of other things to talk about.

"Come on. I want to show you the museum." Mark led the way to an intriguing underground building almost entirely covered by grass. Inside they walked around an atrium filled with plants, studying the animal models and giant skeletons.

Mark stopped in front of a large viewing window toward the rear of the museum. "I worked here for school credit while I was at UCLA."

Behind the glass, a young man in a lab coat was scrubbing bones in soap and water. Nearby, a woman compared one bone after another to animal skeletons on the lab bench. Beside her, a small white sign read: I AM IDENTIFYING DIRE-WOLF BONES.

"She checks them carefully," Mark explained, "because dire wolves, mountain lions, and black bears are all about the same size." He took a deep breath. "It must be a blast to complete the skeleton of an animal no one's ever seen before—to put all the right pieces together for the very first time. Talk about solving a mystery!"

Lucy saw her chance. "How about putting *our* pieces together? We've only got this one day when you're not working."

"Oh, sure. Sorry. We can talk here for a while." He moved farther along the glass wall to watch another woman examine bits of soil under a magnifying glass.

"Okay, we know that Jake didn't switch the snakes," Lucy began. "And we know that he didn't drug Darci's drink. He wasn't even there—"

"For now let's assume the same person did both those things."

"Right. So one suspect is Timon. Well, I know that Timon's bought rattlers from Jerry. He's had to train his horses to work around snakes, which means he's used to handling them. And as for the hoofprints, we

131

know Timon saw the first ones on the trail. Certainly he could round up a pair of bar shoes easily enough."

"Why would Timon have made mistakes in the fake hoofprints close to the road? He's smart and he knows about horses."

"Well, you've knocked out one suspect!" Lucy said with a laugh. "And I've been doing some more thinking about Mavis and Ray. If Darci's right about their motive—that they want to get at her trust fund to keep for themselves—then they have to actually *kill* her! But nothing that's happened really goes that far."

Mark turned away from the glass for the first time.

"Take the pool," Lucy went on. "The insecticide wasn't heavy and atropine is known to reverse its effects. The electric fence was boosted high enough to give someone a bad jolt, but not enough to kill them."

"The snake bite was definitely nasty."

"Yeah. But Jerry told me himself that very few snake bites are fatal, particularly when you can get to a doctor right away."

"So does that dispose of Mavis and Ray as suspects?"

"I think so—that and two other things."

"Did Miss Marple sleep at all last night?"

"Listen, Mark. Mavis and Ray could get at Darci anytime. Why would they mix it up with *Malibu?*"

"Because *Malibu* gave them a chance to hide behind Jake. He was bound to get the blame for everything that happened."

"Not at Van's! And something else about the party. I thought hard about where everyone was standing when the champagne was being poured. Mavis and

Ray had been out on the deck talking to me by the food table. I don't think either one of them left the deck until much later."

Lucy paused and took a deep breath. "What we need is a new suspect."

"Any candidates?"

"Don't be shocked, but yes. I'm zeroing in on Van."

Mark was clearly taken aback. After a moment, he suddenly took Lucy's arm. "Let's go get some lunch. I've got to concentrate on this one hundred per cent!"

They crossed the park to the Museum of Art cafeteria and brought their food to an outdoor table.

"You really surprised me with that one," Mark said as he sat down across from Lucy. "Now spell it out, okay?"

"I haven't found a motive yet, I'm just feeling my way. But start with the drink. Van could easily have doctored Darci's drink and sent it over with Ross.

"I'm sure Van could have arranged the snake switch, too. I heard Jerry say that he'd met with Van a week before the shoot. Suppose Van found out the kind of snake Jerry was going to use. He might even have *seen* the snake. All he had to do was get a matching snake from another animal handler in town."

Mark nodded. "The horseshoes would have been tougher, but Van might have been able to get them from a farrier. Movie directors get away with asking for all kinds of strange objects."

"Something else. The snake went for me by accident when I dropped my crop. It was really supposed to bite Darci. Who but Van could have made sure of that?"

Mark looked at her in a special way. It seemed to mix surprise and respect. "You're right, you know. The director has total control over the situation. Van could have set up the scenes so that Darci was somewhere near the snake and then scared it by accident."

Mark took a bite of his sandwich. His eyes smiled at Lucy. "By the way, while you were running around getting into trouble yesterday, your double told me her part in Van's next feature is a sure bet."

"Oh?"

"She seemed absolutely positive, though she said to keep it quiet. Knowing Darci, ten more people probably heard the same thing."

"Darci isn't going to have much of a career if she only depends on Van. Besides, he was getting pretty fed up the last time I saw them together. You know, I've begun to feel sorry for her. She's really kind of a mess, and it's not all her own fault."

"We're in a funny business, Lucy. In the right part Darci might just take off. Talent doesn't always come into it."

"She's not particularly gorgeous."

"No, but she can be very attractive and sexy when she puts herself together."

Mark seemed to be looking at her speculatively. Lucy could feel her cheeks getting red. She'd forgotten for the moment that she and Darci were look-alikes.

This time it was Mark who broke the mood.

"What about the electric gate? Did Van *deliberately* touch a hot wire to throw everyone off the track?"

"No, I think Jake did the gate and Van was completely surprised. But let's forget that for now. I told you about the trip to TapeDupe, yesterday."

"How does that connect with the rest of the mystery?"

"I wish I knew. So far I'm only sure that Priscilla's the link—Priscilla and *The Little Soldier*. If Dad was right and none of Darci's films has ever been released on video cassette, that copy she knew about was made illegally."

"Of course. But right or wrong, lots of people copy tapes for their own use. There's much more going on here!"

"Lynne and I thought TapeDupe might be *pirating* tapes. Pokey was scared. Someone definitely told him to clam up, I'd bet on it."

"How does this get back to Van?"

"I don't know, but I've had a crazy idea. Priscilla's used to working around cables. It's odd that she should trip. When it happened I saw Van reach out and I thought he was trying to help. But now I'm not so sure."

"You think Van *pushed* her into the pool?"

"Suppose he wanted her out of the way. Not dead, or anything, just off the production. She's a flake I guess, but Slade says she never makes a mistake in her work. Dad wouldn't have agreed to fire her without a good reason."

"Wow, Lucy! Van's a pretty good guy. He'd have to be really cornered to pull anything like that."

"Well, just suppose. Why would Van want Priscilla off the production? If we could figure that out—"

"Maybe it comes back to the tape," Mark said.

"Could Van have heard Priscilla tell you she had a tape of *The Little Soldier?*"

"Let me think." It had been the day of the production meeting. That seemed weeks ago. Lucy felt as though her feet had just hit the ground at the bottom of a slide.

"Mark, I remember it exactly! Van was right there when she told me."

"Now we're getting somewhere."

"Van probably thought if he got Priscilla out of the way, I'd forget about the tape. Suppose, Mark, just suppose Van was selling pictures for video pirating through TapeDupe. . . ."

Mark stared off into space. "Could be. TapeDupe would probably take Van's prints and make masters for Mexico, Turkey—you name it."

"Slade told me Van was down on his luck for a while. He might have needed money. It would be awful to have this come out just when he's made it back to the top. Mark, how would he have gotten the films? From the studios?"

"He certainly could have borrowed his own films a few times."

"This could be awful for my father, if he has to change directors."

"There's plenty of time to replace Van before the next thirteen." Mark pushed his chair back. "We've thought enough for now. Let's have some fun. I want to stop at Power Records, then wherever you say."

Lucy forced herself to go along with the change in Mark's mood. "Could we drive to Venice? I've always wanted to see the boardwalk. Maybe we could roller-skate."

"Sorry, Luce, there isn't enough time. A friend's in a play at the Mark Taper Forum and I've got to eat early. A group of us are going. Do you want to come along?"

"Why not?" she said, trying to sound casual. "I'm supposed to call Dad's office to tell him where to pick me up. I'll check about tonight at the same time."

"Tell him I'll drive you home."

Lucy walked to the phone in a daze. Did going to the theater count as a real date with Mark? Her father was out but his secretary took the message and relayed another. Priscilla wanted Lucy to call her at home between seven and eight. It was important.

"Priscilla's probably furious at me," Lucy said to Mark when she told him about the call.

"Even so, just feel her out. Any scrap of information may help us piece things together."

Lucy thought of the people they'd watched in the museum lab. They were lucky. The pieces they worked with had weight and shape. They ended up with the skeleton of an animal standing in front of them.

She and Mark were fitting a lot of pieces together too. But when they'd done it all, they had nothing to show for it. They still had to find proof.

As though he'd read her mind, Mark said, "You can do it, Lucy. And we'll see this through together." He smiled his brilliant smile.

I take it back, Lucy thought. I've something to show for my effort—one of the best days of my life!

Chapter Thirteen

The play was terrific—a thoughtful protest against nu-
clear war, by a playwright who was only twenty-seven.
Sitting on the edge of her seat, admiring the experi-
mental set and the fine acting, Lucy had been reminded that L.A. was more than sitcoms.

It was hard to turn the play off and to leave Mark's
friends. They'd all treated her as if she were twenty
too. But Lucy had agreed to meet Priscilla in China-
town afterward. There was no problem about Mark's
coming along, and they were both eager to hear what
she had to say.

Priscilla was waiting near the back of the restaurant, her short hair flying, as usual, but her back rigid
and her eyes stern.

"Hello, Priscilla," Mark said warmly as they joined
her at the table. "Good to see you."

"Yeah, thanks, Mark."

"Hi," Lucy said tentatively.

Priscilla merely nodded.

Mark signaled a waiter. "I'm starved. Shall we or-
der spareribs for everyone to start?"

"Sure. And get enough for Pokey too, okay?"

Lucy's eyes darted to Mark but she looked back at Priscilla quickly.

"He's across the street in the car, trying to make sure he wasn't followed. Or you either, for that matter. He'll come in after a while, but he's really scared. That's why we're here."

She glared at Lucy. "I don't know whether to hate you or thank you for meddling in all this. Your visit to TapeDupe raised all the red flags. Pokey'd been warned not to talk about the tapes in the strongest terms. Then when you two waltzed in and asked for *The Little Soldier* . . ." She shook her head.

"Last night I asked Pokey some questions about that video cassette," Priscilla continued. "After a while, he told me a lot more than I expected to hear. I guess he's changed jobs so often he wanted to keep this one badly. He just closed his eyes to a lot of things and did what he was told.

"Anyway, when we talked, he realized that something was going to break loose. I convinced him to meet with you because you could go to your Dad and ask him to help. Whatever happens at TapeDupe, I don't want Pokey caught in it."

"I'm glad my birth sign turned out all right." Lucy said.

For the first time, Priscilla managed a faint smile. "Mark's was better. He's a Scorpio." Once again her expression was guarded. "Here he comes now."

Pokey's round eyes were enormous as he studied Lucy and Mark in turn. He said nothing at all while Mark made the introductions and then ordered some food.

"Tell them about *The Little Soldier,*" Priscilla finally prompted. "Tell them how you got a copy."

Pokey shifted in his chair and played with his chopsticks. "The director brought it in a long time ago—a couple of years, at least. We made a new master from the original print, to send overseas."

"You knew it was going overseas?" Lucy asked with surprise.

"Sure. We took the English speech off the sound track. The new track was just music and sound effects. That's what you do when you're going to dub in a foreign language."

"Did TapeDupe send out a lot of films like that?"

"Enough. I figured the boss had made some kind of a deal with the studios to fix up their flicks for foreign release. Anyhow, I didn't think it was my business."

"And what do you think now?" Mark asked.

"Look," Priscilla said, scowling. "Pokey's telling you all this to get out of trouble, not in deeper. If you're going to be critical, let's stow the talk. So it looks like TapeDupe's feeding masters to video pirates outside the country. But Pokey just worked the dials. He did what he was paid to do."

"It's okay, Prune," Pokey said.

Lucy turned to Mark. "Now the only thing left to figure out is how Van's video pirating ties up with everything else."

Priscilla put down her sparerib. "I don't know how this fits in but I can tell you something else about Van. The truth is, Van pushed me into the pool. He called me over when everyone was very busy. While we were talking he bumped against me so that I tripped over the cable. I reached out to him to catch my balance, but he stepped back."

Lucy felt Mark's kick under the table and tried not to smile.

"I guess he figured he'd better get me off the production so I wouldn't say any more about the tape," Priscilla said.

"Why didn't you tell someone?" Lucy asked.

"Who would have listened? Van had a perfect setup. Everyone was ready to blame Jake for whatever went wrong on the set. They'd have assumed he was after Slade or Mark to delay the production. Why would anyone believe someone pushed me into the water? People trip on cables all the time."

The waiter brought their food and while everyone helped themselves, Lucy thought hard. They'd definitely linked Van to the video pirating and to the pool poisoning. They suspected him of switching the snake and drugging Darci's drink. But what was his motive?

Everyone knew that Darci was after Van for a part in his feature. But that would only be a nuisance. There had to be something else to make him go so far.

"Join the group, Lucy." Mark offered her a bowl of fried rice. "Have some food and let us in on what you're thinking."

"I'm just trying to connect Darci to Van."

"Darci Rutland?" Pokey said. "I met her once."

"Really? How come?"

"She came down to Venice with a friend of mine. Of course I knew her name from working on her films."

"Did you get a chance to talk to Darci?"

"Sure. We all had a beer together."

"So I guess you told her about seeing her old movies."

"I told her I'd done the sound on the masters for overseas. Why not? She was really interested."

"That's *it,* Mark. Don't you see? By accident, Darci found a way to blackmail Van. Only what she wanted from him wasn't money but parts in films and TV shows. If she'd threatened to expose him, Van would have been desperate. He'd be finished if anything like this came out."

Mark's eyes were fixed on hers. "It makes sense! No wonder nothing was lethal. Van's not a vicious man and he's known Darci since she was a little kid. He'd try to scare her, not kill her."

"You two have a lot of big ideas," Priscilla said dryly. "How are you going to prove them?"

"Did Van get copies of the tapes you mastered?" Lucy asked Pokey.

"Yeah. That was one of the things I looked after. I was supposed to make a copy of the original print for him before we erased the English."

"What if we could find one of those tapes at Van's house?" Lucy asked Mark. "We'll be back there for the wrap party tomorrow night."

"That's no answer. Van could say he ran one off for his own use."

Pokey put down his fork. "I'll tell you what to look for. It's called something like *Lucky Penny.* I'll never forget the trouble it got me into. I was new on the job and I didn't understand that the director was supposed to get the complete film. I made him a tape with the music and effects track we sent overseas. Did I get into hot water! But there was nothing to do—he'd already taken the original print back to the studio and he didn't want to ask for it again. If you could find the video cassette of *Lucky Penny,* I think you'd have the goods on him."

Lucy thought of the huge wall of videotapes in Van's study. It would take a long time to check all those boxes. He might not even keep the illegal tapes there. What was that story she'd read in school? *The Purloined Letter.* If only Van agreed with Edgar Allan Poe that the most obvious place to hide something was usually the best.

Mark looked hard at Pokey. "We'll try to find that tape. And we'll try to protect you if we do. But you may have to tell your story to Mr. Hill, or even the police if it comes to that."

Pokey seemed about to turn and run. Then his eyes flew to Priscilla and stayed there.

"Well, I guess," he said after a while. "Prune keeps telling me I never really understood what was going on and I never made a dime from one frame of film. I'll be all right. You just go find *Lucky Penny.*"

The entire *Malibu* unit was at Van's for the wrap party Friday night; the crew, "talent," staff, even the drivers. Lucy watched the cooks at the barbecue pit pull steaming lobsters and clams from the hot coals. Music blared from loudspeakers on the sun deck. Floodlights bleached the sand.

Warmed by the fire, Lucy opened a button at the neck of the green shirt she'd worn for the snake scene. She wondered if Mark would notice that it matched her eyes. Right now he was totally involved in a volleyball game on the beach.

Slade sat regally on the sun deck, positioned as far from the music as she could get. She looked fabulous in a silk print coverall of jewellike colors. Van knelt beside her, talking intently. What would Slade think if she knew the truth about Van? It was odd. Now that Lucy knew the truth, she was surprised to see that Van looked exactly the same.

One of the cooks struck a gong and people began to line up with paper plates. Soda and beer cans popped on all sides. Lucy looked for Mark. They'd agreed to start searching for *Lucky Penny* as soon as the food was served.

The game broke up and Mark made his way straight to her. "We'll have to take turns," he said quickly as Timon headed in their direction. "It will be less noticeable if only one of us is missing at a time."

"Okay. I'll go first. I'll stay about fifteen minutes and let you know how far I got when I come back." Lucy hesitated. "Don't you feel a bit weird trying to pin a crime on Van while we're guests in his house?"

"A little. But I'm not going to waste any time over it. You'd better go," he said as Timon came closer.

In the library Lucy worked out a system. She'd start with the top shelf of the section nearest the door and work her way down. It was a tedious process and she was glad no one showed up to ask what she was doing.

"Start at the second bookcase from the left," she said to Mark back at the beach. "And I think we should open the boxes, too, so we're sure the cassette inside matches the label. Okay?"

Before Mark could leave, Mr. Hill went to the front of the sun deck and rang Van's oriental bells. At the same time a production assistant carried three large cardboard boxes to the Ping-Pong table.

When at least half the group was paying attention, Mr. Hill began. "Ladies, gentlemen—members of the *Malibu* company, gather round. As you know we've managed to shoot thirteen episodes of TV's most absorbing and hair-raising new series. In about six weeks most of us will tackle another thirteen. So that everyone who has participated in this world-shaking accomplishment can be easily identified, step up and give Melanie your size."

Mr. Hill whipped off his sweatshirt to reveal a Knockout of a T-shirt underneath. The *Malibu* logo was in the center, surrounded by Calloway's house, palm trees, the beach, and the Malibu hills.

Minutes later there were Malibu T-shirts on both sides of the volleyball net, around the fire, and dotting the beach. Lucy was thrilled. Now she'd have presents for Allison and Debby that would surely make a hit.

"Your turn. Third section from the left." Mark said in her ear.

Lucy took three shirts back to her room and went to the study. She was dismayed to see a couple making out on the couch. Well, that was that, for now.

As she hurried to report to Mark, Slade called, "Come talk to me Lucy."

"Of course." Lucy sat down beside her. "Are you having fun?"

"In a manner of speaking." Slade smiled warmly. "You'll be leaving us tomorrow?"

"Sunday. And it's going to be hard to get back to school after all this excitement."

"I'm sure. We've got a lot of glitter and glamour out here. But you've seen how much hard work goes along with it." Slade reached for a large handbag on the deck beside her.

"I have something for you, Lucy." She held out a small white cardboard box.

Lucy knew that wrap presents were exchanged at the end of a production, but she hadn't expected to be part of it.

"Slade! I—uh, I don't know what to say."

"Open it."

Lucy lifted the lid and took a slow, deep breath. A silver charm bracelet nestled on a square of cotton. She fingered a silver horse, a riding crop, a horseshoe, a polo mallet . . .

"I don't think girls wear charm bracelets anymore, do they?" Slade said. "But I wanted you to have it. You can see it on my wrist in *Main Line*, one of my earliest films. I played a young debutante who loved horses, and this was a gift from her father. The head of the studio gave it to me to keep."

Lucy kissed Slade on the cheek. And to think she'd been trying to get up nerve enough to ask for an autograph. "I don't know what to say, Slade. It's been so great to know you. I just wish we'd had more time to talk."

"We will. You'll be back. And come to see me— promise! Even if Allan decides I'm getting too old to run my husband's empire, you'll find me on Roxbury Drive, and the welcome mat will be out."

Lucy clutched the little box to her chest. "I think I'll put this away before I lose it, okay? Thanks, Slade, really."

"I hope all your riding dreams come true, darling, and I think they will. You've more than talent. You have discipline and character. That's what it takes. Sometimes I think talent is the easiest part."

Slade looked out at the beach and breathed a deep sigh. "I look at these young people and think how hard it is to keep your balance out here. The technicians are luckier. They don't trade on looks, or that elusive thing called personality. Of course—" She cut herself off, obviously embarrassed.

"Thanks again, Slade," Lucy said and started for her room. Suddenly she had a better idea. She'd take the bracelet to the study and pretend she was looking for a tape of *Main Line*. That would make a perfect cover story if anyone showed up.

This time the library door was closed and no one answered when she knocked. Lucy pushed open the door. Darci was standing in front of the bookshelf shoving a cassette into her purse.

Lucy squared her shoulders and swallowed hard. "Darci, why did you take that cassette?"

Darci's eyes widened, and she said with perfect innocence, "What cassette?"

"I saw you take one of Van's cassettes and put it in your purse. Did he say you could have it?"

"Of course. Why else would I have taken it?"

"You just said there wasn't any cassette."

"I don't think it's any of your business," Darci barked, her face set.

"It's Van's business, though. Why don't I just go get him."

"Do that. I think that's a good idea."

Lucy was taken by surprise. But of course! Darci would be only too glad to show Van that she had proof to back up her blackmail, and if Lucy was standing there, so much the better. No wonder Darci had been so willing to spend the night. It wasn't only to work on Van. It had given her time to scan these shelves.

"I'd like to ask Van how come he has our old films on tape. I know he borrowed a print from the studio once when he was looking for work. My mother knew someone at the company he showed it to. Maybe he made a copy for himself then. But he's got all my movies and I want to know why. I don't get residuals on any of these films. My agent should look into this."

Darci was convincing, but her speech seemed to be speeding up, as though she were rushing a fence.

"You're really a good actress, you know," Lucy said. "But I think I can tell you the real reason you want that tape. To blackmail Van for a part in his feature."

Darci waved a hand and said airily "That's silly." But her mouth contracted into a tight little circle and she pushed past Lucy to get out of the room.

Lucy blocked her path. "It was Van you were afraid of, wasn't it. He was trying to scare you into silence. It started with the drink. Then there was the snake. What tape have you got there, anyway?"

As Lucy spoke, she looked up at the shelves. There was an empty space next to a group of Judy Garland pictures. She took down the next box to the right and opened it.

"Tell me, Darci," Lucy said, casually closing the cover on *Lucky Penny,* "was there any truth at all to that story about Mavis and Ray trying to kill you?"

"What! Are you crazy?"

Lucy heard the door open behind her. She watched Darci's face go rigid.

"Hello!"

It was Mr. Hill.

Lucy kept her back to the door and stared at Darci. "Do you want to tell him, or shall I?"

Chapter Fourteen

Lucy sat out on the Polo Lounge patio at the Beverly Hills Hotel and watched for Mark. Her father was talking on a phone the waiter had just brought to the table. For a minute her eyes wandered to the tall palms behind the sprawling pink building, the lush gardens filled with tropical colors, the perfect green lawns. When she turned back, Mark was walking toward her.

He looked like a star, all right, handsome in dark glasses and a sharp green windbreaker. A small duffle bag hung from his shoulder.

It was probably a good thing that she was saying good-bye to Mark in front of her father. That way she wouldn't get soupy or say anything she'd regret. They'd become friends during these two weeks, she was sure of that. But would they ever see each other again? People often felt close when they were thrown together—on a trip, during a school play. Then when they went on with their lives it didn't last.

As they all said hello, a gorgeous young woman strolled past the table and gave Mr. Hill the eye. Startled, Lucy watched her walk on across the lawn. There seemed to be beautiful girls all around the place like props on a set.

"Well, Mark," Mr. Hill said, when he'd ordered dessert and coffee all around, "I want to thank you for all your help to my private detective, here."

"Would you like to sell us to NBC?" Mark grinned. "Hill and Ladd, Hollywood's hotshot young sleuths." His face turned serious. "Allan, what's going to happen to Van?"

"I'm not sure. He knows he was wrong and I think now that it's all out in the open, he's actually relieved. Van got into a corner when his money was running low, and he couldn't face giving up his house or his Mercedes. He'll get a break by testifying against TapeDupe. He wasn't the only one who brought them films and not too many at that. He'll probably pay a stiff fine. And what he'll hate the most is the dent in his reputation."

"Is he finished in Hollywood?" Lucy asked.

"Certainly for a while. But Van's very talented. All this will blow over eventually. That's the way it goes out here."

"What about Priscilla and the pool?" Mark protested. "What about the snake switch and Darci's drink?"

"No one's going to bring charges. Van's mum about it all and we haven't any proof. Darci certainly won't speak up. Van can accuse her of blackmail."

"I wonder what will happen to Darci," Lucy said. "Maybe without Van to get parts for her she'll work harder at making it on her own. Why can't she try to do a really interesting play at the Mark Taper Forum, like Mark's friends?"

"I think what Darci really needs is a good therapist," Mark said. "I told her so last night."

"You didn't!"

"Darn right I did. It was worth a try."

"Will you use her on any more *Malibu* shows, Dad?"

"Not the next thirteen. They're already worked out." He sipped his coffee. "I should tell you that I had some other news yesterday. The union censured Jake. He won't be able to work for at least three years."

"I guess that's great," Lucy said, "but how will that keep him from wiring fences or making other trouble."

"I talked to a couple of the men last night and they say he's left the state. So I guess that chapter's closed too." Mr. Hill leaned back in his chair. "What's coming up for you, Mark? Anything exciting?"

"You bet. Just what I need before I go back to college next fall. I'm doing a sequel to *Champions of the Gleaming Sword*. I'll get to work in eight different countries and I can't wait. I've been to England and Ireland once, but that's all." He looked at Lucy. "I'll try to go through New York one time and see you. Who knows what kind of a puzzle we can piece together."

Mark reached for his duffle bag and took out a package wrapped in brown paper. "Open it later. It doesn't look so elegant, but I think you'll like what's inside."

Lucy took the package, trying to hide her surprise. Her arm fell to her lap with the unexpected weight.

"Do that, Mark. Come through New York, I mean. I'd really like to see you. And you could meet my brother. I'm sure you two would really get along."

"Of course!" Mr. Hill said. "I'd forgotten that you're both the same age."

They chattered about TV pilots and the networks, Mark's father and Rita, the Angels. Then Mark looked at his watch.

"Sorry, but I've got to run." He shook hands with Mr. Hill. He stopped at Lucy's chair, bent down and kissed her lightly at the side of her mouth. Lucy reached out and held his arm. She could only look into his eyes a few moments before she had to turn away.

"Ciao," Mark said. "I'll write. I'll get your address from the office."

Lucy kept her eyes on Mark until he was out of sight. She sensed her father watching her closely.

"Mite, you've handled this visit remarkably well," he said after a while. "I know it hasn't all been easy."

Lucy could hardly focus on what he was saying.

"This was supposed to be a vacation," her father went on. "It turned into a pressure cooker instead."

She leaned back and turned her face up to the sun.

"But you kept your head." He made a big show of examining one side of her head and then the other. "Yes, both ears are still in place and you're prettier than ever. The sunshine's fixed up that New York pallor. I hate to let you go back."

"I know. I wish I could see Mom and my friends, then turn right around."

"But you like your new school now?"

"Enough. Mostly I'm excited about getting back to work on my riding. From what I've seen so far, I think Oak Ridge will work out. Thanks for talking Mom into letting me go up there."

"I didn't have to talk very hard. I think it's been good for you two to be together without me—and without Eric, for that matter. Mom seems to understand you better now."

Lucy stopped to think. That was probably true. But her mind was someplace else. "I guess you'll be . . ."

"What, honey." Her father's expression was so tender, it only made things worse.

"Nothing."

"You guess I'll be staying out here for good. That's what you were going to say, wasn't it?"

"Right." If she said as little as possible she wouldn't cry.

"I won't lie to you. I am going to stay out here, if things go well for me. But that's the only thing I know so far. Mom and I have a lot to work out and you can't do that by long-distance telephone. I asked her four months ago to come out here for a while. You could have stayed with Aunt Frances. She wasn't willing to do that. . . ." His voice drifted off.

After a few moments, he cleared his throat and went on. "Lucy, you're a piece of my heart. We'll find a way to see each other more. I'll be moving back and forth between New York and L.A. Who knows, maybe someday you'll have a trainer in the East and one in the West too. If we really get lucky, you could even have a *horse* on each coast."

Lucy blinked rapidly. She loved him so much and he was trying so hard.

"I'll be okay, Dad, and it's better now that I've been here. When you don't write, I'll understand better. And when you phone, we'll have more to talk about. To tell the truth, I don't really think I could live here. It just seems too artificial, as though people are showing off all the time. How famous you are and how much money you make seem more important than anything else."

"I don't know," her father said thoughtfully. "It's a crazy town in some ways, I admit. We're in an industry where talent and entertainment come first. Well, you can have a lot of talent without character. There's big money around, often all of a sudden. And when you've so much money that buying a forty thousand dollar car is like sending out for a pizza, you really need character. But there *are* a lot of solid people around here, in the industry and out. Take the faculty at UCLA—"

"Or the volunteers at the museum Mark took me to."

"That's it, Lucy. There are characters out here I'd cheerfully chuck into that La Brea tar pool, but then there are plenty of candidates for the East River back home."

"I love hearing you talk like that. It's a little like me and Mr. Kendrick—I mean Mr. Kendrick and me." She was getting ready to go home, all right.

"Well, I'd better put away my soapbox and you'd better meet Lynne. I'll come to the entrance with you.

155

Shall I take your package and bring it home? It seems too heavy to take along on a shopping expedition."

Lucy clutched the heavy bundle and got up out of her chair. "No, Dad. It's not heavy at all."

Sunday Lucy sat in the back of the limo with her father on one side and Lynne on the other. As the driver put her luggage into the trunk and walked back to the front of the car, Lucy stared at the vine-covered house, trying to take a photograph with her eyes.

"I'm glad you asked me to come along," Lynne said.

"I'm going to miss you both," Lucy said quietly. She brightened suddenly. "Lynne, Dad thought the clothes we bought were terrific. I tried on everything for him when I got home."

"Didn't she look fabulous in the long jacket?"

"And how. I'm going to have a glamorous daughter."

Lucy made a face. "I thought I'd try one or two things with a different look, that's all." Actually, she'd decided to put away some of her *Malibu* money for clothes. She didn't have to be dressed for riding every second of her life.

The car drove through rows of towering palm trees as they left Beverly Hills.

"I don't know which I'm going to miss more, the palms or the mountains," Lucy said. Of couse, it was Mark she'd miss most of all. "Lynne, would you like to see what was in the package from Mark?"

"Of course!"

Lucy reached into the knapsack she would carry

with her on the plane. She pulled the tissue paper away from an ugly round stone that looked like a small gray cannon ball.

Lynne looked confused.

"I was puzzled, too, but look! It's a geode."

The stone had been cut into halves. Lucy took the pieces apart to reveal a magical center of blue and gray crystals.

"It's beautiful Lucy," Lynne said. "You and Mark will stay friends, I'm sure."

Lucy put the stone back beside the note that came with it:

For your treasure shelf. From your special friend in California.

> *Fondly,*
> *Mark*

"Fondly" was better than nothing, particularly from someone as serious as Mark. Lucy thought of Steve, the young painter and riding instructor she'd met this winter at Parkside Stable. He'd been almost twenty, too. And she'd cared about him a lot. When she left the stable, he'd given her a painting of his she had admired.

Maybe she'd start a black book—a list of names of these older guys who were only "friends." A few years from now she'd check them all out and, somewhere, the story might be different.

It had seemed only minutes before Lucy was waving to Lynne and her father from the plane gate. Now, on the return trip, she felt like an experienced traveler. She stepped onto the plane and made her way down the aisle. She stowed her winter coat in the overhead rack, her knapsack under the seat in front of her, and snapped the seat belt in place.

Lucy still felt sore in a few places from the rear and fall, but every black-and-blue mark had been worth it. It was going to be sensational to sit in front of a TV set and watch her scenes with her mother and friends.

As the plane taxied to the airstrip, Lucy wondered if her father and Lynne were watching the takeoff. Her mother, of course, would be waiting at Kennedy Airport in New York. In a way she was lucky. She could go back and forth between her parents. She could take what she wanted from each of their lives. Lucy sat back and closed her eyes. Suddenly she felt as though she had just worked out a tough equation in algebra. The fixed place she'd been looking for was inside herself.

The engines picked up speed and the plane lifted into the sky.

Growing up had always seemed something you reached for over your head, like the top of the Christmas tree when you were placing the star. Today it seemed entirely different—not reaching *up* but *out,* into a larger world.

The problem was not to get swamped by everything out there. Well, that wasn't going to happen. She already had a better sense of herself this Sunday than just two weeks ago. And she'd be thinking over this visit for months to come. Doubling for Darci had been loads of fun, but one thing was sure. In real life, Lucy Hill wasn't going to be anyone's double, *ever!*

Meet Glenwood High's fabulous four, the

SENIORS

Kit, Elaine, Alex, and Lori are very best friends. Every girl's ideal, every boy's dream, these popular seniors share all their hopes, fears, and deepest secrets.

On the brink of graduation and adulthood, they're discovering themselves, planning for the future...and falling in love. Don't miss them!

by Eileen Goudge

_____	TOO MUCH, TOO SOON #1	98974-4-13
_____	SMART ENOUGH TO KNOW #2	98168-9-19
_____	WINNER ALL THE WAY #3	99480-2-18
_____	AFRAID TO LOVE #4	90092-1-17
_____	BEFORE IT'S TOO LATE #5	90542-7-21
_____	TOO HOT TO HANDLE #6	98812-8-27

Laurel-Leaf Books $2.25 each

Judy Blume

Judy Blume <u>knows</u> about growing up. She has a knack for going right to the heart of even the most secret problems and feelings. You'll always find a friend in her books—like these from Laurel-Leaf!

____ARE YOU THERE, GOD? IT'S ME, MARGARET......	90419-6-62	$2.50
____BLUBBER...............................	90707-1-14	2.50
____DEENIE.................................	93259-9-69	2.50
____IT'S NOT THE END OF THE WORLD................	94140-7-29	2.50
____STARRING SALLY J. FREEDMAN AS HERSELF.....................	98239-1-55	2.75
____THEN AGAIN, MAYBE I WON'T.................................	98659-1-15	2.50
____TIGER EYES.........................	98469-6-31	2.95

══LAUREL-LEAF BOOKS══

At your local bookstore or use this handy coupon for ordering:

 DELL READERS SERVICE—DEPT. BR822B
P.O. BOX 1000, PINE BROOK, N.J. 07058

Please send me the above title(s). I am enclosing $_____ (please add 75¢ per copy to cover postage and handling). Send check or money order—no cash or CODs. Please allow 3-4 weeks for shipment. <u>CANADIAN ORDERS: please submit in U.S. dollars.</u>

Ms./Mrs./Mr._____

Address_____

City/State_____ Zip_____